THROUGH THE WRONG DOOR . . .

He screamed once before a cold hand clamped over his mouth. He was wrestled to the ground, his limbs pinned by the frantic mob. He was powerless. He felt their hands moving over him, feeling his body through his clothes, unbuttoning his shirt and his pants. He saw their grinning, maniacal faces, their shaggy matted hair, their filthy hands. Saliva drooled from their gaping mouths as they shrieked and babbled above him . . .

Then he saw the knife.

D1560356

Avon Books are available at special quantity discounts for bulk purchases for sales promotions, premiums, fund raising or educational use. Special books, or book excerpts, can also be created to fit specific needs.

For details write or telephone the office of the Director of Special Markets, Avon Books, 959 8th Avenue, New York, New York 10019, 212-262-3361.

THE BAD ROOM

Christopher Cook Gilmore

AVON
PUBLISHERS OF BARD, CAMELOT, DISCUS AND FLARE BOOKS

THE BAD ROOM is an original publication of Avon Books.
This work has never before appeared in book form.

AVON BOOKS
A division of
The Hearst Corporation
959 Eighth Avenue
New York, New York 10019

Copyright © 1983 by Christopher Cook Gilmore
Published by arrangement with the author
Library of Congress Catalog Card Number: 82-90536
ISBN: 0-380-82669-0

All rights reserved, which includes the right to
reproduce this book or portions thereof in any form
whatsoever except as provided by the U. S. Copyright Law.
For information address Peter Miller, President,
The Peter Miller Agency, Suite 403,
1021 Avenue of the Americas, New York, New York 10018

First Avon Printing, May, 1983

AVON TRADEMARK REG. U. S. PAT. OFF. AND IN
OTHER COUNTRIES, MARCA REGISTRADA, HECHO EN
U. S. A.

Printed in the U. S. A.

WFH 10 9 8 7 6 5 4 3 2 1

To Parker

Chapter One

OWEN VANDERBES drove down Zion Road like a
man in a dream. The day-long drive had dulled
him to a torpid twilit stupor. Mile upon mile of
dense stunted pine and scrub oak crowded the
sandy shoulders of the narrow country road. The
hot dry windstream felt brittle, volatile, about to
combust. Heat waves shimmered from the battered blacktop, tires droned, insects snapped and
splattered on the windshield. Owen shook himself, yawned, and looked around.

In the trees, nailed high among the scrawny
branches, were crudely painted signs. Clipped bits
of Scripture warned and threatened sinners, made
promises in patent truths, bad grammar, and idi-
otic repetition. Owen read heated words about
heaven and hell, God's love and God's hatred, the
Devil, the Mutant, the Freak, and the Fool. He
shook his head.

Poking from the scorched brush were rusted
weed-bound road signs announcing forgotten, hidden towns called Goshen, Jezreel, Pharper and
Beer-Sheba. Owen pronounced the names, looked
at the wooded wasteland, and shrugged. Bored
senseless by the endless jolting over the cracked
and patched macadam, the stale heat of late summer and the timeless, boundless New Jersey Pine

1

Barrens, Owen kept his eyes on the road, but let his mind wander.

He was tired, anxious, and depressed. It was an August heat wave, late afternoon, and he had been driving the old Volkswagen camper since dawn. On the seat beside him sat his six-year-old son, Robin, with a new puppy nestled in his lap. Owen loved the boy and liked the little dog. But in another hour or so he would have to say good-bye to both of them.

They were running late. At noon they had stopped for a picnic and the puppy had run away. They had spent hours running after it, playing a dog's game, and now they were behind schedule. They should have been over the Delaware by now, winding down the shoreline to Lambeth, where Gloria—Owen's ex-wife—was waiting. Owen knew he had better call Gloria as soon as he found a phone. He would have to tell Gloria about the new puppy. There would be an argument.

Since Ephraim he had been looking for a telephone. He had seen auto graveyards, unpainted houses, run-down farms with empty fields, sprawling yellow gravel pits. He had passed deserted diners, defunct, rotting farmstands, small, shallow lakes, and bogs of stagnant, brown cedar water. He had gone by the Little B Bar, which was closed; and the Bonanza, burned down. To Owen, who had driven it often before, Zion Road was a recurrent nightmare. He swore to himself, sweated, and kept an eye out for a place to make a call.

"I don't think this doggy likes me," said Robin. It was the first thing he'd said in an hour.

"Sure he does."

"Then why did he run away?"

"Well, he didn't run away. He just ran, that's all."

"Why did he run, daddy?"

" 'Cause he's a pup and pups love to run. Especially Doberman pups. Did you see him go? Six weeks old and he runs like a racehorse."

"But he could have got lost, daddy. He could have gone away forever."

"He didn't, did he? He could have, but he didn't. When he got tired he let us catch him."

"What do I do if he runs away again and you're gone?"

"He won't run away."

"What if he does?"

"He's not going to. See, once he's been around you awhile, a week or so, he'll get used to you. You keep him on the leash when you walk him and he'll get used to that. And then, when you let him loose, he won't run away. He'll run, but he won't go far. You'll see."

"I don't know, daddy."

"You'll see."

"Do you think mommy will let us keep him?"

"She better."

"I asked her if I could have a kitty and she said no."

"She did?"

Robin nodded. "She said no cats."

"Your mother doesn't like cats. But she'll like that dog. You'll see."

Robin shook his head. "Mommy said no cats and no dogs."

"I'll talk to her."

"What if she says no?"

"Well . . . she's the boss. But what I think is

3

that she'll like the dog if she sees that you like it. You do like it, don't you?"

"I guess so."

"He's awful cute, Robie."

"Yeah."

"And wait till you see him when he's grown up. A Doberman is a beautiful dog. And very smart, too. He'll be your best friend."

"He bit you, daddy."

Owen rubbed the two red dots at the meaty base of his thumb. The pain went away.

"He didn't mean to. He just got scared when I grabbed him."

"You swore when he bit you."

"I said ouch."

"No you didn't. You said God damn son of a bitch."

"I did?"

"I heard you, daddy. God damn son of a bitch."

"That's enough of that, Robie."

"I'm telling mommy."

"You better not."

"I'm only kidding. I won't tell her anything."

"Yes you will. She'll want to hear all about your vacation, everything we did. You tell her how much fun we had."

"I don't want to go home."

"Yes you do."

"No I don't. I want to go back with you, daddy."

"I'd love it if you could, Robie, but you can't. You know that. You've got to start school . . ."

"I could go to school where you live."

"No. Not now. But maybe someday."

"When I'm older?"

"When you're a little older."

"How much older?"

4

"We'll see."

"Daddy?"

"Yes."

"Why did you run away?"

Owen exhaled. "I didn't."

"Sure you did." Robin was beginning to cry.

Owen put his arm around the boy and hugged him. Keeping his eyes on the road, he spoke softly. "Okay. I ran away. I'm sorry."

"Why did you do it?"

"I don't know."

Robin stared out the window.

"We were arguing all the time, Robin. We were making each other unhappy."

"Why?"

"I don't know. Maybe it was my fault. I can be very obstinate."

"What's obstinate?"

"Stubborn."

"That's what mommy said. Stubborn."

"She did?"

Robin nodded, patting the dog.

"I don't quit, Robin. When there's something I have to do, I do it. I don't let anything stop me. I think that's important."

Robin rubbed his eyes.

"I don't think it's wrong to believe in something even if nobody else believes in it. The things you believe in come right from your heart. Listen to your heart; nobody else."

Sulking, Robin said nothing.

"Look at me. I'm a boat-builder. I'm practically the last boat-builder on the Jersey coast building boats out of wood. Everybody switched to fiberglass, everybody told me to switch to fiberglass. Including your mother. But I believe in wood,

Robie. I think a wooden boat is much, much nicer than a plastic one, and I don't care what *anybody* says. See?"

Robin nodded.

"The wood I use comes right from these woods, most of it. Jersey cedar. White oak. Best wood in the world for a boat. And look at it all, thousands of miles of woods right in the middle of the most crowded state in America. Funny people living in here, too. Pineys. A lot of the families go back to the Revolution. . . ."

Owen looked at his son from the corner of his eye. There was a certain look that came over the boy. It was coming over him now.

"Hey, Robie, think about this: in a few years we'll build you a boat. A skiff. We'll fit her out with mast and sail. Spruce mast, cotton sail, just like the old days. We'll put a dagger board in her so she can be dragged up on beaches and mud-banks. And when we get used to her we'll sail her down the coast to Cape May and then up the Delaware. We'll sail her all the way to Lambeth and show her to your mother. How's that?"

Robin shifted in his seat. His eyes were vacant, unfocused, dry.

"Come back, Robie."

There was no answer. Robin had withdrawn and would not return until some secret inner switch was thrown. Owen did not know how to throw the switch, but he kept trying.

"Hey! What are we going to call the dog?"

Robin shrugged.

"Dog's got to have a name, Robie. Let's think one up. It's your dog, so the name should come from you. Any ideas? . . . Let's see. . . ."

A dark shadow crossed the road. Owen looked

at the sky and saw thunderhead clouds. Anvil-shaped, they were flat and dark at the bottom, billowy and white at the top where the sun peeped through. Thunderheads meant summer storm, heat storm, with plenty of wind and rain. Maybe it would hold off.

A huge bug splashed wings, legs and yellow matter on the windshield. Owen pushed the spray button, but nothing happened. He turned on the wipers, but they just smeared the mess across the glass. The goo turned Owen's stomach, but he didn't stop to clean it. Owen didn't like the Pines. He'd grown up at the seashore, and the woods and the people who lived in them were a mystery, a threat. As long as he kept moving he was only an observer, not a part of the Pines, not under their sinister influence.

The day had been like one of those dreams where you have to do something vital and you can't get started, where the harder you try the more impossible it becomes. The storm clouds were filling the sky and the light was dim, shadowed, cool, like the light in dreams.

Owen's depression deepened, his anxiety increased. Something was very wrong with Robin. Little Robin, sitting like a statue, holding on to his horrible, numbed silence, was in trouble. He had nightmares, he wet the bed, he bit his nails, he wept bitterly and often. He hadn't enjoyed his vacation. Right there by the sea, he'd spent most of his time in front of the television set. Robin couldn't get through a day without ten hours of television.

Owen blamed himself for his son's distress. It had started the year before, just after the divorce, and it was getting worse.

7

"Hey, why don't we give him a German name? We could call him Manfred or Helmut."

Robin stared straight ahead.

"Jesus, Robin, can't you answer me, say something?"

"I don't think this dog likes me."

Robin covered his eyes and cried quietly.

Owen stepped on the gas.

A small sign, set close to the road, caught Owen's eye. On it were freshly painted Gothic letters reading:

PUT MY MOTHER IN ANOTHER MATRIX

Owen read it, yawned, and frowned. A hundred yards farther another sign appeared, then another and another, forming a poem. As Owen sped by he read the lines to himself.

PUT MY MOTHER IN ANOTHER MATRIX
PUT MY BROTHER IN ANOTHER JAIL
PUT MY SISTER IN A HOME AND KISSED HER
PUT MY FATHER IN THE U.S. MAIL
DON'T NEED A COMPASS TO FIND ORION
DON'T NEED MY NEIGHBOR TO FREE MY SLAVE
DON'T WANT A WOMAN TO FEED MY LION
BURMA SHAVE

That was new. Owen had been driving Zion Road for two years to visit Robin, and he'd never seen the poem. Somebody had painted over the old Burma Shave signs. But who had done it, and why, and what did it mean? Every other sign along the road was about God, the Devil or vegetables. Owen shook his head and tried to repeat the poem, but it was gone. He was still thinking about it when he passed the sign for Mizpah.

"Jesus. Mizpah," said Owen.

"What's Mizpah, daddy?"

Owen looked at Robin and smiled, happy to see him coming around.

"Far as I know it's just what you see from the road: a bar and a fire tower. Look ahead, you can see the tower now."

Up the road, looming above the Pines, a tall wooden tower reached up to the boiling black clouds. Bright sunlight flashed momentarily on the windows at the top, as if the watchtower were winking, signaling.

"What's a fire tower?"

"There's a man up there, looking for fires in the woods. When he sees a fire he calls the firemen."

"I bet you can see everything from up there," said Robin.

"What's to see? Miles of pine trees. Miles and miles and miles. Drive you crazy. Hey, there's the bar. I wonder if it's got a phone."

A roadside bar, close to the base of the fire tower, was centered in a small, empty gravel parking lot. It was called Sooey's and it looked open. Owen hit the brakes.

Robin and the Doberman pup looked out the window. Sooey's was a single-story frame building with imitation brick siding, boarded-up windows and a cedar shake roof outlined in broken neon tubing that had once glowed red and green. It looked like every other bar in the Pine Barrens. An unpainted door was ajar, a ruined screen door hung from one hinge over a rotted wooden stoop. In the parking lot was a Budweiser beer sign, and painted on it in Gothic letters was the one word:

Sooey's. It was a Piney bar, miles from nowhere, drab and dreary, but it looked open.

Robin glanced at his father and frowned. The dog looked nervous, alert.

"If I don't call your mother she'll kill me."

"Okay." Robin yawned and stretched.

"Want to come in for a Coke?"

Robin shook his head. "Can I sleep in the back?"

"Sure. Hop in the back and get some sleep. I'm going in there, make the phone call, and I'll be out in one minute, okay?"

"Okay."

Robin crawled over the front seat and lay down on the wide bed. The camper had curtained windows all around and the light was bright and cheerful inside. Owen had done it all—built the bed, the table, the shelves for the stove, pots and pans. Everything was wood and Owen was proud of it.

He moved the camper to the shade by the bar and killed the engine. He got out and stretched, listening to the woods. It was calm, peaceful, and a pine-scented breeze blew softly. He peeked into the back of the Volkswagen and smiled. Robin was asleep with the dog curled up by his feet. Owen wished he had a camera.

There were no cars in the parking lot, no traffic on Zion Road. Sooey's was silent and still. Owen remembered the watchtower.

Looking up, he had to crane his neck and shade his eyes to see the top. Way up there, behind thick panes of glass, someone was watching everything. Up in the tower, like God himself, someone had the overview.

Owen didn't like it. He felt out of his element,

10

cut off, vulnerable. Something was telling him to get back in the camper, to go while he could.

But then he remembered Gloria. Maybe a phone call would soften the landing, make things right; maybe she'd be nice and they'd have an evening like old times. Maybe she would forgive him, and Robin would forgive him, and he would forgive himself.

Owen walked into Sooey's like a fool stepping off a mountain.

Owen found himself in total darkness.

"Anybody here?"

He heard a hand come down heavily on wood, then a woman's voice.

"Sure as hell is! What do you want?"

"I need to make a telephone call."

"Right there on the wall."

"Can you turn on some light?"

"Plenty of light! Your eyes just ain't used to it. Come in and set and you'll see fine."

The only light in the barroom came from a small black-and-white television set at one end of the bar and a glowing Budweiser beerwagon display at the other. The air smelled of cigarettes, stale beer, and the bathroom. Owen, standing just inside the door, waited dumbly for his eyes to adjust to the gloom. He could barely make out a low, painted ceiling, yellow plaster walls, and a black linoleum floor.

He found the phone, dialed and waited. A male operator with a nasal voice came on the line, saying a brushfire near Tabernacle had taken out a telephone line. He said if Owen would wait a moment or two he would ring him back with the connection.

11

Owen didn't want to wait. He wanted to get out of Sooey's and find another phone. But wouldn't every Piney bar on Zion Road be the same? Sooey's spooked him, but maybe he was being irrational, paranoid. He agreed to wait for the call. He hung up, nodded in the direcion of the bar, and walked back outside. Robin was sleeping soundly, just as he had left him.

Owen leaned on the camper and sighed. God, he loved the little boy! Just looking at him made him feel good. After today he wouldn't see him except one Sunday a month, until next summer's vacation. And if Gloria got mad enough he wouldn't even have Sundays. Owen shook his head sadly and walked back into the bar.

"Over here," said the woman, "and watch it you don't trip on Dee."

"Dee?"

"Dee, the dog! Get it? Dee for dog!"

"I can hardly see a thing, ma'am," said Owen.

"You been in the sun too long, is all."

He took two high and cautious steps, banged into a bar stool, centered it, and sat down. Sooey's was coming into view: dusty bottles on plywood shelves, a brass cash register with an open drawer, and the woman. She was short, stocky, and gray-haired. Her broad face with its pointed chin and nose had once been attractive. She mopped her way down the bar to him, smiled and fluttered her eyelashes. Her eyes were dark, deeply set, penetrating.

"I'm Rose," she said, "but you can call me Dusty."

"Good afternoon," said Owen.

"What's on your mind?"

Owen looked toward the door. Little Robin was

12

okay in the camper. Owen had time for a beer, one beer, just to calm him down, make him right for the phone call.

"A bottle of Budweiser."

"Glass?"

"No, it's okay."

She bent over the beer box, rummaged through ice, water, and bottles. Fishing a bottle from the dark tank, she held it to the light of the TV, looked at the label from an inch away, and shook her head. She put it back and chose another. Owen heard the cap hit the floor and the bottle tap the bar. He drew a bill from his pocket, looked closely, and saw that it was a five. Dusty took it from his hand and made change. Owen brought the bottle to his lips and drank with his eyes closed. When he opened them Dusty was perched on a wooden stool across the bar from him. She leaned forward and winked.

"Got relatives here?"

"Where?"

"In the asylum."

"What?"

Dusty looked down and tapped her long fingernails on the bar, a tap for each word.

"Mizpah Insane Asylum," she said.

"Where's that?"

She nodded toward the door. "See the fork by the fire tower? Just up that fork a quarter mile."

"I never heard of it."

"You ain't from around here, then."

"I'm from the coast. Upstate."

"I get a few customers in here got relatives in the asylum. Not too many, though. You're hardly ever allowed to visit anybody in there."

"This your bar?"

13

"Just the last twenty-five years."

Owen took a sip of beer and tried to look at the television, but the screen was a white blur.

"I was born in Gath and raised in Askelon. In the Pines. Both them places are gone, but us Sooeys is still going strong, huh?"

"Looks like it," said Owen.

At that moment a rear door opened. Through it came a young man bearing a thick book. He had large eyes and blazing red hair. He was thin, pale, and anemic-looking, with bloodless lips and a bony body. His features were fine and delicate. Despite his milky coloring, or because of it, he was a very good-looking young man.

"When did you get home?" asked Dusty.

"Just walked in, ma."

"I didn't hear no bus stop."

"It didn't. I just jumped out the window on the way by."

"I'd appreciate a straight answer, Rupert."

"I walked in from Michmash. Through the woods."

"You was in the lake?"

Rupert shook his head. "To the library. Got this book and took two back. Want to hear something?"

"I got a customer."

"I'll read it to you later."

Rupert walked to the far end of the bar, climbed onto a bar stool, and began reading his book by the light of the Budweiser display. Dusty, her eyes on him, poured herself a shot of whiskey and drank it. She refilled her shotglass with beer from Owen's bottle. Owen stared at the phone.

"That's my boy," said Dusty to Owen. "It's just the two of us here."

14

"And Dee," said Owen.

"Yeah, Dee."

"Where is Dee?"

"Out for a pee!" said Dusty, laughing and slamming the bar. "One hell of a dog, Dee. Mostly hound. Though he's awful nervous for a hound. I don't know that I can believe he is one."

"Nervous?"

"Crazy's more the word. Gun-shy, scared of the woods, scared of people. Most I can say about him is he's a good dog."

"Behaves himself," said Owen for something to say.

"Better than some people do," she said, casting a glance at Rupert. Rupert looked up, then down at his page. He turned it slowly, carefully.

"Dee don't bark," said Dusty.

"Hounds aren't supposed to bark," said Owen. "They bay."

"Dee don't make a sound, hee hee. Never gets underfoot. He don't fight, he don't bite, he don't fart, and he don't shit in the yard. That's all I can say."

"I've got a dog," said Owen.

Dusty picked up Owen's beer, squinted at it, and threw it into a trashcan behind her. Without asking, she opened another, taking money from his change. Owen wished the phone would ring and he could get back to his boy.

"What kind of dog *you* got?"

"Doberman. A pup. Just got him."

"Plenty of Dobes around here."

"There are?"

"Up the asylum. Guards use 'em to keep the loonies in line."

"I'll bet they do."

15

"What'd you get a Doberman for?"

"For my boy. He picked him out of a pet shop."

"Got a boy, huh?"

"Six years old."

"Me too. I got Rupert there, sixteen, and I got a daughter, Ruth, ten years older." Dusty swallowed another shot and added, "She's in Mizpah."

"Beg your pardon?"

"She's in the asylum. That's what folks around here mean when they say 'Mizpah.' They mean the madhouse. Around here 'Mizpah' and 'loony bin' is one and the same. For Christ's sakes don't tell nobody you had a beer in Mizpah; they'll think you're rats in the attic."

By the pale blue glow of the Budweiser Clydesdales, Rupert put a thin finger to a line in his book, looked directly at Owen, and spoke:

"The Lord watch between me and thee when we are absent one from another."

Owen and Dusty peered at the boy through the gloom.

Dusty asked, "What was that?"

"Genesis."

"Reading his Bible," said Dusty, winking.

"It's not a Bible," said Rupert, holding up the heavy book. "It's called *Bartlett's Familiar Quotations*. It's a reference book, but they let me take it out."

"What was that you read us?" asked his mother, again winking at Owen.

"That line's called the 'Mizpah Benediction.' But you could call it a malediction, since it was also a curse. Anyway, Mizpah means 'watchtower' and not a goddamn lunatic asylum, see? It's what I wanted to read you."

"Rupert's first in his class over at Canaan Regional," Dusty said to Owen. "Going to be a preacher."

"Hell I am."

"He's thinking about it."

"I'm an atheist," said Rupert.

"No he isn't."

"I'm the only atheist in the Pines."

"He's kidding."

"Everybody thinks I'm nuts."

"No they don't."

"Hey, ma, every day I go to school somebody makes a crack about Mizpah. Nobody'll come near me."

"Hell with them," said Dusty.

"You ought to hear the kids when the school bus lets me off. They go crazy! Even the bus driver gets nervous. Nice place to live, huh?"

"That's enough, Rupert. This man here is waiting for an important phone call—"

"Listen to this," said the boy, flipping to a turned-down page. " 'Had there been a lunatic asylum in the suburbs of Jerusalem, Jesus Christ would infallibly have been shut up in it at the outset of his career.' Havelock Ellis."

Dusty slapped the bar with her bar towel. "I said that's enough, boy."

"Bear with me, ma, I got one more. Wordsworth. 'We poets in our youth begin in gladness; but thereof come in the end despondency and madness.' Maybe I'm right where I belong, huh?" Rupert grinned.

Owen raised his eyebrows as a thought hit him. "Do you write poetry?"

Rupert looked suspicious. "Sometimes."

"Did you write the one out there on Zion Road?"

"There's a lot of stuff out there on Zion Road."

17

"The one on all the little signs," said Owen.

"Burma Shave."

"Yes."

"I wrote it," said Rupert. He put his nose back in his book and went on reading. Dusty continued to stare at her son, shaking her head.

"Everybody's crazy," she said.

"What?" asked Owen.

"The men are nuts and the women are cracked!" She pounded on the bar and howled with laughter. Owen forced a smile.

"Speak for yourself," said Rupert.

"Hey, who asked you into this conversation? The man and me are having a talk and you nose in. Just nose out."

"You're nuts," said Rupert.

"I'm nuts? Listen to him. He's the one who's nuts, I can tell you. Talks to himself night and day—"

"She tell you about Dee, mister?"

"Shut up."

"Dee the dog? Good ole Dee? Well, there isn't any Dee. *Dee don't exist!*"

At that moment the phone rang.

"Gloria?"

"Putting your call through," said a voice. The phone was ringing on the other end. Owen closed his eyes, blotted out Sooey's.

"Hello." Voice flat, irritated.

"Gloria? It's Owen. Everything's okay."

"Thank God. Where are you?"

"We're on the road. We got held up, but we'll only be another hour or so."

"Another hour? You were supposed to be here at three."

18

"I'm sorry Gloria; we really did get held up."

"*How* did you get held up?"

"It's really a funny story. I'll tell you when I get there, okay? You'll love it."

"Owen, right now I'm supposed to be showing waterfront to a minister and his wife. A very big deal for me, Owen. And instead, I'm sitting here waiting for you. What the hell happened that's so funny?"

"If I tell you now it'll ruin the surprise."

"Ruin it."

Owen took a deep breath. "Okay. Only let me finish before you get mad."

"Christ, Owen, just tell me."

"Gloria, he spent the first week with me in front of the TV. I mean day and night, breakfast, lunch, and dinner. The beach right outside his door, plenty of kids to play with, lots of things I wanted to do with him. And all he did was watch the tube. Commercials, soap operas, everything, anything."

"It calms him down."

"It makes him like a zombie, Gloria."

"The doctor wanted to give him tranquilizers, Owen. I figure TV's better."

"What did he say is wrong with him?"

"They never say. Finish the story."

"I got him a dog."

There was a long, flat silence.

"Gloria, it snapped him out of it! He plays with the dog, he sleeps with the dog, he talks to the dog."

"No."

"Huh?"

"I said no. No dogs."

19

"Gloria, I tell you I've made some kind of contact with him, and you're making up rules—"

"Don't start."

"I'm not starting—"

"Owen, listen to me. I'm trying to run a business, my own business. It's a lot of work, but I love it just like you love your work. I'm away all day. I come home exhausted. Robin's in school all day, eight hours. I make him dinner, I put him to sleep. Where do you fit in a dog?"

"I'll take care of everything! I'll build a doghouse and a run. I'll pay for all the shots, food, license, everything."

"No dogs."

"Gloria, it's a cute little Doberman puppy. You'll—"

"Keep it."

"It's *his,* Gloria. I gave it to him."

"No way."

"Will you just think about it?"

"You still haven't told me why you're not here."

"Ha! Wait till I tell you. We, ah, stopped and had a little picnic—just me, Robin, and the pup. We were eating sandwiches by a little stream, having fun. Then the dog got away. Loves to run, loves to play. I don't know how long we spent running it down, half the afternoon I guess. And you know what? Robin was laughing the whole time. Laughing, Gloria. How long since you've heard him laugh? Not since before—"

"Owen, it's a phase. Kids go through it when their parents split up. It'll pass."

"You don't think it's serious?"

"No."

"Jesus, Gloria, you got to be blind not to—"

"Owen, I've got another call. Hold on."

"Don't put me on hold! I got to get out of here."

"Well, get out, get going, and get here. No dogs."

"Gloria—"

"I have a *deal* on the other line, Owen."

"You're not going to do this to my boy!"

"Owen, you start talking like that, you might as well hang up."

"God damn it, Gloria!" Owen slapped the wall, clenched his fist.

She'd hung up on him.

"Cool off," said Dusty, as Owen returned to the bar.

Owen's throat was dry, constricted, choked with emotion. He sighed and sat down, his hands shaking. Dusty poured herself a shot, drank it, and went into a coughing fit. When she recovered she thumped her chest and smiled crookedly.

"Great burn," she said. "Want one?"

Owen nodded, his mind a blank. Dusty poured, filling a shotglass to the top.

"Reminds me of the stuff Rupert's daddy used to make," she said in a stage whisper her son couldn't help but overhear. Owen downed his shot and rose to go, but Dusty put her hand on his and held it.

"He was a gypsy moonshiner," she said. "He had a truck with a still in the back that made booze from almost anything. We were making it from apples up in Jericho, then we came down here and made it out of pinesap. My God, it was pure ethyl."

At the far end of the bar Rupert riffled the pages of his book. Owen wanted to go, but Dusty held on.

Her whisper sounded like boots crossing over gravel. She watched Rupert as she spoke.

"We used to sit out there in the pines and sip that stuff when it was hot. A glass would kill you! But we'd just sip us a wee bit and lie back and watch the moon go over."

"Making it all up," said Rupert.

"Bullshit," said Dusty. "Was when you were a baby, so you wouldn't know."

"Don't believe a word she says, mister," said Rupert, returning to his book.

Dusty raised her whisper. "That pinesap whiskey made us both batty, I swear to God it did. But it was like magic! It changed everything. One minute I was froze-ass in the pines, next I was snug in the arms of my gypsy moonshiner. Sweet Jesus, we sang all night."

"Bull," said Rupert, pronouncing the word carefully.

Dusty changed her whisper so that it sounded like stones dropping in wet sand.

"We caught my Ruthie sipping that stuff. Only thirteen, she was. Pretty, but wild. Wild!"

"I've got to go," said Owen.

Dusty made Owen's change slowly, then turned back to him.

"They didn't take my Ruthie away, mister," she said. "*I* put her away. I signed the papers all those years ago and she's there still."

Owen fumbled for his change, saying nothing.

Dusty's whisper was low now, like rocks rumbling on the bottom of a stream.

"Know why I did it?"

Owen stared at Dusty. A gleam came into her eye.

"I caught her being naughty. *With her daddy.*"

22

Then she winked, nodded her head toward Rupert, and waited.

There came a tremendous crash. Rupert, raising his heavy book high over his head, brought it down full force upon the Budweiser beerwagon. Plastic horses and beer barrels scattered everywhere, crunching under Rupert's feet as he stood.

"Liar!" he screamed, running for the door. As he threw it open, a flash of lightning turned the dark bar to daylight. He screamed something over his shoulder, but it was drowned out by rolling thunder. Then he was gone.

"So long, Dusty," said Owen on his way to the door.

She didn't answer.

As Owen stepped onto the gravel parking lot a heavy rain began to fall. He ran to the van, yanked open the door, and jumped in. Fumbling through his pockets for the keys, he called over his shoulder to his son.

"Sorry I took so long, Robie. You okay?"

There was no answer.

Just then, from far off in the woods, came a long lingering wail. The wail turned to a scream—a woman's scream, or a young man's. Then there was nothing but the hard rain.

Owen's blood ran cold. He hoped Robin hadn't heard the scream. He turned, peering into the darkness behind him.

"Robin?"

No answer. Owen snapped on a light.

The boy was gone.

Chapter Two

OWEN ROLLED DOWN the window and shouted against the rain: "Robin!"

The rain drummed on the roof of the camper, harder now. Thunder crashed, rolling over the black sky. Owen leaned on the horn, turned on the headlights, screamed.

"ROBIEEEEE!"

Nothing.

A hot flash passed over him like heat lightning over an open field, and he began to sweat. He blew the horn until Dusty appeared in the doorway.

"What's going on?"

"My boy's gone!"

"Mine too," she said, peering into the woods where they were lighted by Owen's headlights. "One hell of a night for it."

"Lady, he's *six years old!*"

"Jesus."

"ROBIEEEEEEE!"

They both waited. Nothing.

"Maybe he's up the watchtower."

"What?" asked Owen.

"The watchtower!" she said, pointing to the wooden structure that sat just beside the parking lot. "Maybe he went up there!"

Owen calmed himself, thinking hard. They'd

talked about the fire tower, the view from up there. Maybe Robin hadn't been able to sleep. Maybe he'd gotten bored waiting. Maybe he'd climbed up all those stairs before the storm. He'd be up there now, waiting for his dad to come and get him. Maybe.

The top of the fire tower was seven stories from the ground. Owen ran up the first three flights, two steps at a time. He had to stop and catch his breath. His hands clutching wet wood, he slumped against a heavy oak beam and watched lightning slash viciously at a dark and endless sea of pinewoods.

Owen tried to run, but gave up after a few steps. The best he could do now was a slow halting climb, one painful step at a time. He was soaking wet and choked for breath, his heart beating at twice its normal rate. He felt old, clumsy, heavy, weighted down by the rainwater in his hair, his clothes, his skin. He crawled up the last two flights on his hands and knees.

At the top was a narrow catwalk, exposed and slippery, with flimsy wooden railings that sagged outward. Five more steps led to a trapdoor beneath the observation room. His head reeling with vertigo, Owen kneeled on the top step and pounded on the trapdoor.

He heard slow and heavy footsteps overhead, the door opening. A brilliant light flashed in his eyes. He tried to speak, but was too weak, too winded to make an intelligible sound. Mouth working, eyes rolling, tears of rage and frustration falling from his cheeks, he gestured frantically with both arms, waiting for his voice to return.

The light went off. Without warning he was kicked in the face.

The blow sent him sprawling backward onto the wet catwalk, leaving his head hanging over the edge, seven stories from the ground. Painfully he rolled to his stomach, grabbed a rotten railing and hung on. A voice from the darkness above him shouted above the storm.

"You're on State property, you drunken son of a bitch! Go back to Sooey's." The trapdoor slammed shut.

Owen lay still for several minutes, catching his breath, feeling his face to see if his nose and teeth were broken. They were not. When he was sure he could speak he shouted up at the trapdoor.

"I'm not drunk! I'm looking for my son!"

He heard low laughter, two men speaking, no reply.

Robin wasn't up there.

Owen looked down, saw Dusty in her doorway peering up.

"Call the police!" he shouted.

"Phone's dead!" she shouted back.

Owen groaned, tried to think. There wouldn't be another phone for miles. He heard Dusty shout from below.

"They got a radio up there!"

Owen crawled up the steps, pounded on the trapdoor.

"For the love of God, listen to me up there! I'm not drunk . . . I'm—"

He was given no time to finish. The door sprang open and a hand grabbed him by the collar, lifting him upward. A nasal voice spoke evenly, asking a simple question.

"You one of those guards from the asylum?"

26

Owen moved quickly. In the darkness he felt for the man's wrist, found it, and squeezed hard. Using only the thick, callous fingers of his right hand he applied pressure until the man screamed. He could have broken bones easily, but he did not. He ground them slowly, one against the other, while the man shrieked in agony and went limp. Keeping his grip, Owen crawled up and over him, through the trapdoor and into a darkened room. A light came on.

A high, squeaky voice called out, "Oh Jesus, mister, don't hurt me!"

"I won't hurt you if you'll listen to me."

"Let him go!" said a tall stout man in a ranger's uniform. His pink face was contorted with panic and fear.

Owen looked down. The man he held was a ranger—fat, bald, and over fifty. He was quietly sobbing, completely limp. Owen took off some of the pressure and waited while thunder roared and rolled away across the Pines.

"My son. He's six years old. Is he here?"

"No, sir."

"Then he's out there somewhere. I've got to call the police. Now, you either let me use your radio, or I won't just hurt your friend . . . I'll kill him."

"I'll do anything you want me to."

"Okay." Owen released the ranger and stood up, looking around him. The room was large, walled by heavy glass waist-high to the ceiling. In the middle was a large square table and on it a sighting device for locating forest fires. In a corner were instruments, including a shortwave radio set. Owen pointed to it and told the ranger to call the police. The man on the floor behind him stopped sobbing, dried his eyes.

27

The ranger made the call, requesting the State Troopers. When he finished he turned to Owen.

"You got to understand us, mister," he said. "We thought you was a drunk from Sooey's. We get them all the time. Then we thought maybe you was a loonie from the nuthouse, see? We got a goddamn nuthouse a quarter mile away. You can understand, can't you?"

Owen nodded.

"Couple weeks ago we had some drunks out of Sooey's try to set us afire, right, Bob?"

Bob was sitting on the floor, nursing his wrist. "Last year we had a guy try to throw Bill right off the tower," he said.

"Put the Troopers on him," said Bill.

"Six months they gave him."

"State property."

"You wouldn't know it. People around here think a fire tower's open to the public."

"If you could call them people."

"Pineys," said Bill. Then he looked at Owen. "You from the Pines?"

Owen shook his head.

"Fuckin' Pineys," said Bob.

"Scum."

"Backward, ignorant . . ."

"Crazy."

"Out of their fuckin' minds, mister. Inbreeding."

"You only got to look in their eyes."

Owen grunted, looked at the rangers. Both Bob and Bill had large bloodshot eyes. Bob had a facial tic and Bill's hands trembled. Their noses were bloated and veined from alcohol, their cheeks pitted. Their age, shape, and mannerisms were nearly identical. As they spoke they looked out

the windows, not at Owen. There was never a
moment when one of them wasn't watching the
woods.

Owen looked out the windows. Lightning
cracked, thunder roared, and the whole room
swayed with a tremendous blast of air. The tops of
the pines were moving like a field of black wheat,
like waves over a black sea.

"You think your kid might have gone in those
woods?"

"I don't know."

"God, I hope not," said Bill.

"Not tonight," said Bob.

"Not any night. Or day," said Bill.

Owen stared at the woods.

"There's a story about a man went in there, a
doctor, and lost his way. Was in broad daylight.
He was just takin' a walk in the woods."

"He was a hunter, Bill."

"No he wasn't, but it don't matter. It wasn't
here he went in; it was a place five miles up from
here, up by Tabernacle off Route 40. He took a
turn off the road, parked the car, and left it. He
was walkin' along and he got onto one of them
deer trails."

"Not for a human bein'," said Bob.

"No, sir. As he found out. He followed one of
them deer trails that lead to nowhere, then he got
lost. The trail just ran out on him the way they do.
A deer will sometimes barge into the brush and
not go anywheres. Just lookin' for a safe place to
sleep. He barges in there till he can't go no farther, then he lays down and sleeps."

Watching the woods, the rangers were calm, in-
tent. Owen was waiting only for the Troopers, half

listening to the story. It was a story he didn't want to hear.

"So this doctor goes in and gets himself all caught up in there like a fly in a web. It was the brambles, and he couldn't get out, couldn't even move around much."

"Terrible thing," said Bob.

"Mister, when they found him he was all dried out and dead. Hands and arms cut through to the bone and creatures all over him."

"Stop it," said Owen.

"That's the end of the story."

"Good."

"Well, I just meant that the sooner they find your little kid the better for him."

"I know."

"Tell him about the cats, Bill."

"It's common knowledge, mister."

"What is?"

"We got a problem around here with cats."

"Snakes too."

"Christ, yes, but the cats is the worst. Used to be a lady had a cabin up Zion Road."

"The cat lady," said Bob.

"She was from Camden, but they put her out of Camden because she had too many cats. This woman had over a hundred cats, most of them with one disease or the other. They moved her out of Camden and put her down here."

"What a stink."

"Mister, you could smell her place from miles away. She lived alone, naturally, and she was batty as all hell. Somebody killed her."

"Pineys."

"You can bet on it. She got killed and nobody knew about it. When the food ran out, the cats ran away. They started living wild, in the woods."

"A cat can do that, mister, not a dog."

"Yes, sir. A cat can live wild. They can fend for themselves in the wild. But the thing is they get mean. I mean *mean*. And the kittens grow up even meaner."

"And bigger."

"Tell him, Bob."

"They'll attack a man. Tear him apart."

"It's happened, tell him."

"It wasn't here, but it had to be these cats. Over by Pomona is the Air Force base. The guards have to stand duty in the woods. All night. There was a guard, a young fellow. He had a .45 and a night-stick. He was walking around and he ran into a pack of these cats. They tore him apart."

"Tell him what they did to him."

"I don't want to hear it, okay?" said Owen. "I'm very upset."

"You ought to be."

"Did you know there's more rattlesnakes right here in the Pine Barrens than any other part of the U.S.?"

"Timber rattlers."

"We got a skin down in the shack seven feet long."

"Seven feet, mister, and a rattle big as a man's cock!"

"I mean the *sooner* they find that boy—"

Owen slammed his hand down on the table, causing both rangers to jump.

"Look," he said, "we'll talk some more when the Troopers get here, okay?"

"I got nothing to say to them," said Bill.

"Me neither," said Bob.

"You just let me know when they're here," said Owen.

"You'll see 'em."

"Hey, you know what, mister?"

"What?"

"Maybe they already got him. He might have met somebody and got turned in."

"They didn't say anything when you called, right?"

"No."

"They never do. Not on the radio. They're real careful about what they say over the radio."

"Motherfuckers."

"What have you got against the State Troopers?" asked Owen.

"They think they own the Pines."

"Think they're God."

"How do you mean?"

"The State Troopers," said Bill, "were formed to patrol the state highways—the turnpike and the parkway. They're traffic cops and that's all. But what's happened is they've started to run things in all the little Piney towns that don't have no cops, see? Everybody's scared shitless of them."

"They ain't local, see?"

"And they're all big. You got to be six feet to be a State Trooper."

Owen was five feet six inches tall. He was short, but he was thick. He weighed 225 pounds and it was all muscle. Owen was built like a fireplug.

"You got to have blond hair and blue eyes to be a Trooper."

"No you don't."

"Seems like it."

"Don't let 'em push you around, mister."

Owen sighed. He found the flashlight and snapped it on.

"You mind turnin' off that light?"

"Why?"

"So's we can see better."

"We're on lookout. You got lightning, you got pines, you got fires."

Owen turned off the light. Bill put his arm around Bob. The two rangers scanned the woods.

"Want to see how we locate a fire?"

"No."

"Called in a hundred nineteen fires this year."

"And it's only August."

"Had two yesterday."

"Woods are dry."

"It could rain all night and they'd still be dry."

Just then Owen saw a light in the woods. It was not far away, perhaps a quarter of a mile. Squinting, he saw a car's headlights moving slowly among the trees. The rangers were looking the other way.

"What was that?" Owen asked, pointing to where he had seen the headlights. The rangers stared in silence. A light came on, a light in a window, pale yellow.

"That's the nuthouse," said Bill.

"Mizpah," said Bob.

"I just saw a car's headlights in there," said Owen.

"Huh?"

"I saw a car."

"By that light there?"

"Yes."

"That'd be the doctor," said Bill.

"What doctor?"

"Alvin. He runs the place. He *owns* it."

33

"That's a bad place, mister."

"It's a hospital, isn't it?" Owen asked.

"If you say so. But you don't go there to get well."

"You don't?"

"You go there if you killed somebody, mister."

"Killers in there, buddy."

"You mean it's a prison?"

"Might as well be. Walls and bars."

"Do they ever escape?"

"Nope."

"Never?"

"Not that we ever heard. We been here nine years."

"Tell him about the dog, Bill."

"He don't want to hear it."

"Let me hear it."

"Well, that old bitch down there, Miz Sooey, she had a dog."

"Dee?"

"Dee what?"

"Was the dog named Dee?"

"I don't know what the hell the dog's name was, mister. I never have a word for that old bag. I got this story off the Troopers. That dog wandered off one day and went into the nuthouse. Broad daylight. Squeezed through the bars in the gates. Wasn't a big dog."

"Black and white dog."

"Medium-sized, black and white like Bob says. Anyway, the loonies in there got hold of it. A bunch of 'em was out in the yard when the dog came in and they snatched it."

"They ate it," said Bob. He turned his head.

"They ate the dog," said Bill. "Alive."

Owen put both hands to his temples, shut his

eyes, and squeezed. Waves of fear and nausea passed over him. The rangers were quiet and there was only the sound of the storm, the furious wind and rain that beat against the fire tower until it trembled.

"Hey, look there, Bill."

"I see 'em."

"What?" asked Owen.

"State Troopers. Comin' up Zion Road."

"Better get to ground level, mister."

"Watch yourself with those bastards, huh?"

Owen let the trapdoor slam behind him.

He was standing in the rain when the squad car pulled into the parking lot. The driver, a young, blond-haired and blue-eyed Trooper, removed a pair of yellow sunglasses as Owen approached.

"You the man who lost his kid?"

"Yes. Did you find him?"

"Negative. Want to get in the backseat?" As he spoke the rear door swung open. Owen got in the car. Another Trooper, young and dark-haired, turned and faced him, unsmiling. He squinted, studying Owen's face. He asked questions and his partner wrote things down on a yellow pad. He called Owen by his first name.

Just then a large yellow Chrysler turned off the road and stopped behind the squad car. A tall heavyset man in uniform got out and stood in the rain, hands on his hips. The Troopers studied him in the rearview mirror. The driver got out, walked over and exchanged words with the newcomer. When he returned he was soaking.

"That's Chief Howzer, Owen. He'll want to ask some questions when we're finished."

"Okay."

35

"You all right?"

Owen was trembling. "I'm very worried."

"That's understandable. Tell me something. Do you have any idea what could have happened to your boy?"

"I . . . I think he's lost."

"You think he ran away?"

"No."

"Just went for a walk?"

"I don't know. I guess. Maybe the dog got away and he went after it. Maybe he just went for a walk."

"You think somebody might have taken him?"

"Oh Jesus, I don't know."

"You didn't see anybody else around here?"

"No."

"You didn't hear a car?"

"No."

"How much have you had to drink today, Owen?"

"A beer! Two beers, maybe. I'm not drunk. I—"

"Calm down, Owen."

"Okay." Owen clasped his hands to keep them from trembling. Suddenly he wanted to get out of the squad car. He noticed there were no locks on the rear doors, no handles for the windows. He was a prisoner.

Chief Howzer's face, massive and lined, appeared in the front window. Both Troopers stiffened.

"That your man?" he asked, nodding in Owen's direction, but not looking at him.

"Yes, sir," said both Troopers at once.

"What's he think?"

"He was in the bar, Chief. He don't know what happened."

Chief Howzer looked at Owen. He shook his head.

"What kinda name's 'Vanderbes'?"

"I asked him. It's Dutch."

"Where's he from?"

"Seabright."

"Where the hell's Seabright?"

"It's on the coast, Chief. Up by Long Branch. Monmouth County."

"And what's he doing here?"

"He says he was on his way to Delaware. Taking his kid back to his ex-wife. He's divorced, wife has custody."

Owen leaned forward, shouted, "Let me talk to him. I—"

"What's he saying?" asked Howzer.

"Wants to talk to you."

"What's the matter with him?"

"He's upset, Chief. He's afraid for the boy."

"Has he got booze on his breath?"

"Yes sir."

"Get him out."

"Sir?"

"I said get him out of the car. Then go check out Sooey's. *Move.*"

Chief Howzer's mouth was set in a hard thin line. Rain fell from his visor, coursed down his weathered cheeks. He looked into Owen's frightened, staring eyes, then at his hands.

"Put your feet together."

"What?"

"I said put your feet together. Stand at attention."

Owen put his feet together, his arms at his sides.

"Put your arms out. Close your eyes."

Owen followed orders.

"Touch your nose with your right forefinger."

Owen brought his finger to the tip of his nose. Keeping his eyes closed, he did it with his other hand.

"I said your right hand, God damn it."

Owen opened his eyes, looked at Howzer with hatred.

"Show me where you left him."

Owen walked to the camper, slid open the rear door. "He was on the bed asleep. I left him here while I made a phone call to his mother."

"You locked the door?"

"No."

"Why not?"

"I didn't think to. There was nobody around."

"So he could have climbed out if he wanted to."

"Yes."

"And somebody could have climbed in if they wanted."

Owen's head swam. He leaned against the camper until he was steady.

"Don't get excited, Mr. Vanderbes. I don't see no footprints. I don't see no tire tracks. But the rain could have washed them away. But somebody, some nut, might have stopped and seen your kid and snatched him."

Owen's head snapped up. "I saw a car!"

"When?"

"I was up the fire tower there, waiting for you. I saw a pair of headlights. They were right next to the . . . the asylum."

"I'll check it."

"I heard terrible things about that place."

"Bullshit. That's one place that's never given

38

us any trouble. What you heard was superstition."

"Will you check it?"

"I said I would."

"When?"

"When I'm damn good and ready, Mr. Vanderbes."

"What are you going to do now?"

"I'm going to question Mrs. Sooey. I'm going to question her son. I'm going to question her. Then, when I'm through talking to everybody, I'm going to talk to *you.*"

"Talk to me now. Ask me anything you want."

Howzer held a finger before Owen's nose and said evenly, "I told you what I'm going to do. You're going to go back in that squad car and sit tight."

"Am I a suspect?" Owen lowered his voice.

"You sure are."

"Why would I steal my own child?"

"Maybe you got a reason. Maybe you don't have a reason at all. Maybe you're *nuts,* Mr. Vanderbes."

"What?" Owen spun around.

"Calm down."

"You think I'm crazy?"

"You're shouting, Mr. Vanderbes."

Owen lowered his voice. "Chief, since I stepped through that door there I've been with very strange people. In fact, everybody I've met is totally wacko. But *I'm* not. I'm upset. My son is missing. He might be lost out there in those woods, with the cats, with the snakes, with the . . . he might have been kidnapped. I have to *do* something. Do you understand? I have to go look for him."

39

"You move out of my sight and I'll put you in custody."

"You don't understand."

Howzer was furious. He looked away, spat into the rain. He looked at his car and back at Owen.

"I don't believe a fuckin' word you've said, buddy. I think you're drunk or nuts or both. Now you get your ass in that car and shut up."

"I'm going to look for my boy, Chief."

"You are going no—"

At that instant Owen slammed his fist into the Chief's stomach. Chief Howzer's eyes crossed as he went down, settling slowly like a balloon, the air knocked out of him. Helpless and gasping for breath, he could do nothing as Owen stepped over him.

Owen hid behind thick bayberry bushes until he heard the squad car pass by on Zion Road. He waited for the Chrysler, but it didn't come.

"ROBIE!"

Crickets stopped their chatter, then continued madly. The boiling night sky, bordered by the black wispy tops of pitch pine, rolled and raged above. Wiping sweat from his eyes, Owen watched the black clouds scramble across the heavens like a herd of clumsy animals in panic. Stabbing a finger at the pale moon, he whispered, "Where's Robin?" It was the closest he could come to prayer.

Ten yards ahead of him a young wild-eyed doe stepped onto the road, saw Owen, and turned back. Crickets screamed in a cacophony of insect frenzy and mosquitoes began their attack. The rain turned to a drizzle and stopped.

Owen thought he heard something moving in

the woods to his left. Moonlight fell on a narrow pathway leading into the pines.

"Robin?"

Deep in the woods there was a rustling sound.

"Robin!"

The sound was repeated.

Owen took the path. Plunging into the woods, driving himself through the dark brush, he missed a turning and slammed headlong into the trunk of a rotting birch. A heavy wooden sign fell from the dead branches above, striking Owen's head. Stunned, he fell to his knees. Bright points of light circled before him and the pain was great.

The sign lay near him, its face to the ground. Groaning, Owen turned it over and by moonlight read the hand-lettered message:

THE LORD THY GOD IS A ANGRY GOD

A few feet from him something made a sound. Defensively Owen held the sign between himself and the noise. Peering over, he saw the eyes of a small dark animal looking directly at him. The creature came forward slowly, submissively lowering its head.

It was the dog, the little Doberman. Owen's breath came out in a long anguished sigh. He held out a finger and the puppy licked it.

"Where's Robin?"

He stared desperately into the yellow eyes of the dog and the dog stared back.

It was very simple. Robin had let the dog out of the camper. The dog had run into the woods. Robin had gone in after it and had gotten lost. The dog was here. Robin could not be far.

"Robin!"

The dog jumped, turned, and walked away. Owen followed, certain the dog would lead him to his boy. Deeper into the woods they walked, the dog moving in starts and stops, keeping ahead, Owen bent low.

They came to an open place where the path crossed deep car ruts in the soft earth. Without hesitating, the dog turned to the right and ran along a muddy track. Owen ran behind, his hopes building.

The dog knew. Obviously the dog knew exactly where it was going, knew it was leading father to son.

The puppy disappeared around a curve, then reappeared, excited by something, waiting for Owen to catch up. Owen ran hard, panting and out of breath, but running hard. Suddenly, before he could stop himself, he smashed into the side of a parked automobile. He crumpled to the ground.

Pulling himself to his knees, he waited for his head to clear. Looking about him, he made out a half dozen cars parked in a rough circle, all of them facing the center. In the middle sat the dog, staring eagerly at Owen.

The car he leaned against, an old Buick, was missing its hood, trunk lid, and wheels. The glass from the windshield, windows, and headlights littered the sandy ground with shards that sparkled in the moonlight. Bullet holes and gashes from shotgun blasts appeared in the doors and fenders, and a horrible stench rose from the dark interior.

"Robin?"

Rusted chrome grilles smiled at him with broken teeth, stared at him with blasted eyes. The cars were in ruin—scavenged, vandalized, brutalized, desecrated, decayed. Owen was in a Pine Barrens auto dump, a muddy end of the road for cast-off, driven-into-the-dirt, forgotten wrecks, silently commiserating under the moon. Owen felt like one of the cars.

"ROBIEEEEEEE!"

The little dog bolted at Owen's scream. It collided with a Ford station wagon, turned and slunk under a burned-out Dodge.

A hand to his ear, Owen turned in slow circles, waiting for any sound of his son. But all he could hear were the insects—the ecstasy of the crickets, the mania of the gnats and mosquitoes. Bloodthirsty, they lighted on Owen's skin and bit him unmercifully.

Shivering, the dog crept from under the car and came near. Owen knelt and tried to pat its head. The Doberman ducked away. Owen grabbed a rear leg. The dog turned and bit his hand.

It was no more than a nip, but it frightened Owen. It was a warning, and Owen would remember. He held out his fingers, but the dog stayed away.

"Where is he?"

The puppy walked directly to a path Owen had not seen. It hesitated, looked back at Owen, turned its head to one side, and made its strange Doberman puppy sound. Owen got up and followed.

The path was wide, clear of branches, and well used. The dog skipped along and Owen ran behind, both of them picking up speed. Then, without warning, the path ended. Owen plunged headfirst into the deep water of a stagnant cranberry bog.

Thrashing wildly in the black water, Owen

screamed for help. The water closed over him, rushing into his open mouth and throat. Touching a muddy bottom, he kicked to the surface where the image of the moon lay floating, jeering at him. His hand touched leaves, twigs, the end of a thin and brittle branch. Owen grabbed and held on.

In a few minutes he caught his breath and pulled himself to shore. There was no bank, only a snarl of brush, shrubs, and thorn. The path he had taken was lost somewhere in the darkness. The dog was gone.

He crawled through the brambles, forcing his way forward with all his strength, standing erect when he felt solid ground. Though the dense brush blocked him and tried to hold him, he barged forward. He tore at the weeds with his hands, drove aside the thorns with his shoulders. After ten minutes he had gone twenty feet. He was exhausted, weak as a child, unable to move in any direction. He sank to the ground with a shudder. He was trapped. He was lost.

The mosquitoes found him quickly. They attacked his face, neck, hands, and ankles. They bit him through his wet clothes. They bit and they stung, they sucked his blood and went mad in his ears. Owen tried to drive away his agony and despair.

"ROBIEEEEEEEEE!" He sobbed, tried to call again, gave up.

There was no answer; his little boy was nowhere near. The little black demon of a dog had led him into a trap and abandoned him. The Pines had him like a bug in glue. The cats and the snakes and whatever else the woods harbored would soon be on him.

Suddenly, with a stab of bitter anguish, Owen

realized that he'd made a mistake. Instead of his desperate, frantic, futile search, he should have stayed with the Troopers, with law, order, and people who knew the Pines.

Owen cursed himself, God, and the woods. He sobbed, buried his face in the wet rotting leaves and reeking mud. Something stung him viciously on the back of his neck, drawing his blood, but Owen was too worn out to slap it away.

Everything was against him. The people, the Pines, the animals, and the insects were in league. He was being punished for his sins, his selfishness, and his stupidity. God and nature were mocking him, jeering at his impotence, listening with indifference. It was as if he were some laboratory animal, the center of a cruel experiment, the object of some inhuman research.

And it was just beginning.

Chapter Three

OWEN WAS half out of his mind from the mosquitoes when he heard a voice. The sound was not far off, somewhere in the darkness just ahead and to his right. The sound stopped and there were only the crickets in the brush, the mosquitoes in his ears. But then it came again. It was a song, a nursery rhyme, whispered, chanted:

Dance with the dolly with the
   hole in her stocking, hole in her stocking,
   hole in her stocking.
Dance with the dolly with the
   hole in her stocking,
Dance by the light of the moon!

Owen called for help.
"Hello?" answered the voice, faint, cautious.
"Help me! I can't find my way out of here!"
"Come ahead."
"Where? I don't know which way!"
"Just come toward me," said the voice. "You're not far."
Owen began to crawl in the direction of the voice. Worming his way through the snarled vines, thorns and creepers, he moved around things he could not tear or force aside.

"Come on," said the voice quietly. "You're almost to me."

"Where?"

"Keep coming."

Owen broke through a snarl of chokeberry brush, stood, tripped, and rolled heavily into an evil-smelling drainage ditch. On his hands and knees he crawled up the bank to a narrow gravel road. In the pale moonlight he could see no one, but he knew he was watched. Panting, filling his lungs with fresh air, he tried to calm himself, ready himself for the stranger.

On the road the mosquitoes were even worse. But now he was free to brush them from his face, neck, and arms. He caught sight of his hands. They were cut and bleeding, smeared with black mud and brown water. They were numb, detached, foreign-looking, like a pair of old gardener's gloves. He held them under his arms and tried to stop trembling.

"Who are you?" The voice came from the dark brush on the other side of the road.

Owen, still kneeling, turned toward the voice, raised his hands. "I'm looking for my little boy. He's lost."

A tall thin figure stepped out onto the road, keeping a distance. "You're the man who had to make the phone call," it said.

Owen could see the milk white skin, the flaming red hair. "You're the kid," he said.

"Rupert. Remember?"

"I remember. Owen."

"You all right, mister?"

"I'm in a terrible jam."

Rupert crossed the road, squatted in front of

Owen, ran his hand through his red hair, and asked what was the matter.

Owen told him everything.

"You punched Howzer?" Rupert's long red hair shimmered as he laughed. Owen didn't laugh.

"I was just very upset. I still am. I don't know what to do."

"Just calm down. Relax."

"I've got to *do* something."

"Don't go back in the woods."

"I won't."

"Boy, I wish I'd been around when you hit Howzer. By tomorrow that'll be all over the Pines!"

Owen looked at Rupert. The boy was dry.

"Where were you? Where'd you go?"

"I went in the woods."

"Jesus," said Owen. "The woods."

"I'm good in the woods."

"Where'd you go when it rained?"

"There's old cars in there. I just picked one."

"Christ," said Owen.

"Glory," said Rupert.

"Rupert . . . my little boy . . . is out there in the woods somewhere." Owen's voice and hands were shaking now.

"He'll be okay, Owen. Calm down."

Owen shook his head slowly. "I was out there. I wasn't okay. I almost lost my mind."

"You made it. He'll make it."

"I'm a grown man. Robin is six years old."

"Does he get scared easy?"

"No."

"He'll make it."

Owen lay on his back on the macadam. He tried to think. Instantly he became conscious of a terrific throbbing at his temples, an ache at the base

48

of his skull, and pains in his muscles and bones. He was exhausted, yet his heart raced. He lifted his head and let it fall back to the road. It felt good. He did it again, over and over, matching his heartbeats with bumps on his head.

"You're making me nervous, Owen," said Rupert.

"Sorry," said Owen. He stopped.

"It's okay."

"I just don't know what I'm supposed to do next."

"Think."

"I'm trying to."

Owen closed his eyes and tried to think. He was flat on his back under a black sky filled with stars and one huge yellow moon.

"Car coming."

"What?"

"Quick, hide. Car coming." Rupert dashed to the drainage ditch. Owen followed on all fours.

Headlights, then the sound of tires on the gravel road. Chief Howzer's big yellow Chrysler cruised by slowly.

"Hey, Owen, that was the Chief!" said Rupert with a huge grin, pale thin lips, ghost white teeth.

"Where's he going?"

"Only one place you can go on that road."

"Where?"

"The *madhouse*." Rupert pronounced the word carefully, softly.

"Okay. That's where I'm going," said Owen. "I'm going to check out those headlights I saw." With direction, with something to do, Owen felt better. He stood and began to walk.

"Owen?" Rupert said from behind.

49

"What." Owen didn't turn around or stop walking.

"Can I come?"

Owen looked back at the boy. Rupert's pale face glowed in the moonlight. It was a sad, wise, sensitive face, full of hurt, ready for more.

"I think you better go back," said Owen.

Rupert caught up. A foot taller than Owen, he looked down at him and said, "I can't go home."

"Why not?"

"I'm locked out."

"How do you know?"

"It's after dark. I'm locked out."

"Your mother will let you in."

"No she won't. It's after dark. Dusty's drunk, passed out. The fire tower could fall on her and she wouldn't wake up."

Owen didn't know what to say.

"So maybe I'll just go along with you," Rupert said.

"I'm going to the insane asylum."

"You said."

"I'm a fugitive now, Rupert. If they catch us we'll both go to jail. Or worse."

"I don't care."

"Do you know the way?"

"Sure. This road leads right up to it. It's a kind of a driveway."

"Where does it start?"

"Back at my mom's bar on Zion Road. Right where you started, only you went the hard way, through the woods."

"I'd still be in there if you hadn't come along."

"You sure would."

"Okay, Rupert, we'll stick together."

"The road curves just ahead. That's why it's so dark."

"You've taken this road a lot?"

"Many times."

"At night?"

"Sure."

Rupert swung in beside Owen and together they walked the moonlit road to the madhouse.

"Your mother said your sister's in the asylum."

"She is."

"I guess you see her on visiting days."

"Nope."

"Why not?"

"Not allowed. I'm a minor and a minor's got to be with an adult. And Dusty won't go."

"She won't?"

"Ruthie won't see her. She won't have anything to do with Dusty. So there I am."

"Do you write to her?"

"Yes."

"Does she write back?"

"Yup."

"Then you know her a little."

"I know her."

"Is she . . . all right?"

"Well, she's as good as she can be under the circumstances. She's under lock and key. She's cooped up with some real maniacs. But she doesn't complain."

"It's terrible to have someone you love . . . in a place like that."

"Horrible. Have you ever had to put somebody away?"

"Yes."

"Who?"

"My father. He's in an institution."

"What kind of institution?"

"It's an old-age home, up north."

"Do you visit him?"

"No. I used to go. But they said it upset him when I came. He doesn't know me. The last time I went he thought I was a doctor. So I don't go."

"Was he a good father?"

"He was a wonderful father, Rupert. The kind you look up to."

"What did he do?"

"Same as me. He was a boat-builder. He built big skiffs for fishing, commercial and pleasure. At one time he had forty men working for him. Forty men. I grew up in his boatyard. I was doing a man's work by the time I was ten. He taught me everything."

"Is that what you do now?"

"Yes. And it's all I want to do. Of course, it's a lot different now from what it was. Commercial fishing's tapered off and fiberglass boats have taken over everything. I make wooden boats."

"What kind?"

"Specials. Yachts, fishing boats, pulling boats. I build on orders. I make surf boats for all the beach patrols up and down the coast—the ones that still want wooden boats. And I make sportfishermen, twenty-five to thirty-five foot. Single engine, twin engine. All wood."

"What kind of wood?"

"Teak, mahogany, oak, cedar, fir, pine—you name it."

"Sounds like hard work."

"I like hard work. I'm cut out for it."

"You look strong."

"Rupert, I was born strong. When I was five I

could bend nails. I could bend a silver dollar now, if I wanted to."

"You could?"

"You bet. I'm short, but I'm strong. When you're young and you're built like me, you get in fights. People want to try you. I never lost a fight. Never started one, either. And I'll tell you, when you work around wood you better be strong. You turn your body into a machine. I don't like most power tools. I like my hands, my arms."

"Do you have many men working for you?"

"Two."

"That's all?"

"Well, like I said, fiberglass has put a big dent in the wooden boat trade. Everybody I know has gone over to fiberglass."

"How come you don't?"

"Because wood is better. I like wood, I grew up around wood. I like the way it works, the way it smells, the way it looks. My father taught me things, beautiful things that are lost today. I'm going to teach them to Robin some day if . . ."

Owen's mind drifted to thoughts of his son. Rupert brought him back. "Did you go to college, Owen?"

"Yes."

"I'm going to go to college."

"What are you going to study?"

"Literature. Poetry."

"Do you write a lot of poetry?"

"I read it a lot. I write some."

"What's that one about that ends with Burma Shave?"

"It's more of a joke."

"It doesn't mean anything?"

"Well, sure it does."

53

"Then what's it about?"

"About me, my family, all the madness."

"Madness?"

"My theme."

"Why?"

"Why what?"

"Why so much craziness?"

"I guess because I've seen so much of it, growing up in a bar."

"That's drunkenness, Rupert."

"What's the difference?"

"Well, when you get drunk you go crazy. But when you wake up the next day you're okay again."

"Not the drunks I know. They wake up crazier than ever."

"I see." Owen listened to their footsteps on the loose gravel, the crickets, the mosquitoes.

"Did you like college, Owen?"

"I didn't want to go. When I got out of high school I just wanted to work for my dad. But he insisted. He didn't want me to build boats."

"Why not?"

"He wanted me to be a doctor."

"A doctor?"

"He knew I wasn't going to make much money with a boatyard. By the time I was your age he was down to a dozen men. Five years later he had four old guys who would work cheap because there was nobody else who would hire them. He knew what I'd be up against, trying to make a living like he did."

"What happened?"

"I went to college, but I never made it to med school. I studied philosophy for four years. The main thing I learned was that I didn't want to be a doctor. I wanted to build boats, that's all. And when I know what I want to do, nothing stops me."

"That's the way to be."

"It's what my father told me: don't quit, don't give up. If you really want something, you're the only person who can get in the way."

"Right."

"When I graduated I came home and asked my father for a job. We had a fight and things were never the same again. Then, when my mother died, he fell apart. He gave up; he quit."

"Too bad."

"Yes. Well, you can't blame the man. Something in his head clicked off. I think the doctors did it to him."

"The doctors? How?"

"He was upset about my mother's death. The doctors gave him drugs, tranquilizers. That's when he really changed. The drugs took all his strength, his willpower. He couldn't help himself. So he changed. He turned into this docile, helpless old man. I'll never let that happen to me, Rupert. *Never.*"

"Me neither."

"When my father went to the hospital I took over the boatyard. I got married, had Robin."

"Then what?"

"I got divorced."

Rupert shrugged. "What else is new?"

"Your father's divorced?"

"He's dead."

"Tell me about him."

"What do you want to know about him?"

"I don't know."

"He was nuts about chain saws. He had seven chain saws. What in hell do you do with seven chain saws? I'll tell you what you do: you go to work on the trees. He cleared the parking lot and couldn't stop himself. He went for the backyard. Used to be nice and shady in the backyard until dad went to work on the trees.

"One day I was lying in bed, looking through a crack in the wall. There were two silver birches out there then, saplings, very beautiful and healthy. I used to love to look at them through the crack, watch them grow a little each day. Then, one day as I'm looking at them, *buzz buzz.* I hear dad coming. I hear the chain saw buzzing and I know what's going to happen. *Blip, blip,* and over the two of them go."

"Why would he do that?"

"He was nuts. Oh God, was he nuts. It was that shit booze he made. Gypsy moonshiner, my ass. He was just a crazy old fart from Philadelphia. Only Dusty would have picked him. You only had to take one look at him to see he was bats. He pointed a gun at me once."

"He did?" Owen watched Rupert from the corner of his eye.

"He was gun-crazy too. He had half a dozen handguns and some deer rifles and shotguns. One time we all went into the woods—me, Dusty, him, and a woman from the bar. All drunk except me, naturally. I'm around ten years old at the time. He was showing off, showing us how he could move through the trees like an Indian, without making any noise. And he was making a hell of a racket, believe me.

"Then he got going so fast we lost him. Or he lost us. So we had some fun in the woods. Dusty and the woman had a bottle, and I recited some poems for them. Then we headed back to the bar.

We found him sitting on the porch with a twenty-gauge shotgun and a bottle from the bar. He was crazy drunk and pissed off and none of us knew it. I came up on him and he raised the gun. Pointed it right at me, finger on the trigger, told me he was going to blow me in half." Rupert stopped walking.

"Why?" Owen looked up at the boy.

"Said I ditched him, ditched him in the woods. Said I was out there in the woods having fun with his wife and his woman."

"Jesus. That's terrible." They went on walking.

"Jesus Christ, Owen, his own son."

"What did you do?"

"It was real quiet. Dusty and the woman aren't saying a word. Dad's got his finger on the trigger and he's got a look in his eye like he's never seen me before. Everybody froze except me. Me, I wasn't scared, I swear to God I wasn't. I figured if I got scared I'd run. And if I ran he'd get me in the back."

"Jesus."

"I gave him the dumbest smile I got. I pushed the gun away and sat down next to him. I asked him for a swig of whiskey. I'd never taken a drink before and he hated me for that. So when I asked him for a drink he got so happy that he put down the gun and handed me the bottle. Dusty took the gun away and we all pretended it was a big joke."

"Was the gun loaded?"

"Loaded and cocked, Owen. Safety off."

"My God. What happened to him?"

"He was a time bomb, a living time bomb. He finally blew himself up."

"How did he do that?"

"I told you he liked guns. He never went hunt-

57

ing; he just liked to play with them, take them apart, put them together, shoot them off in the backyard. He got into loading, loading his own rounds. He got himself a loader and a scale and all that shit and he loaded his own. Near the end, what he liked to do most was sit on the back porch, drink whiskey, load shells, and smoke cigarettes. Everybody told him he was going to blow his head off."

"Did he?"

"He blew it off."

Owen gulped, putting one foot before the other on the gravel road.

"We never found it, Owen. Probably out there in the woods somewhere. Stuck in a tree, maybe."

"That's horrible."

"Blown to pieces. A living time bomb. I'm just glad he didn't take us all with him. It's happened around here. My seventh-grade math teacher shot his wife and four kids. He wounded the dog, a shepherd, but the shepherd got away. Then he shot himself through the mouth. I think my father blew himself up on purpose."

"Why do you say that?"

"He was a miserable man, a weak, crazy man, and he drank to forget what kind of a man he was. He wasn't like you, Owen. He was weak, a quitter. He gave up."

Rupert held out his hand, whispered, "Hold it, Owen, we're here."

Before them stood huge iron gates set in a high wall that ran through the woods. The gates were black, rusted, and heavy, with sharp spikes at the top that curved inward, away from Owen and Rupert. Above the spikes, in rusted wrought iron, was one word: MIZPAH.

Just then, on the other side of the gate, a car appeared. Owen and Rupert ducked into the trees. They heard someone fiddling with a lock and chain, the gates swinging open. Through them moved Chief Howzer in the unmarked yellow Chrysler. He was alone.

When the car had passed through, the gates swung shut, the padlock clicked. Owen saw a gray uniformed shape tug the chain once, then move away into the shadows. He saw a dog, then another, poke their snouts through the narrow bars, then move away. They were fully grown Doberman pinschers, brown, black, and big.

"That's what I saw," whispered Owen. "When I was up in the fire tower, during the storm, I saw headlights on this road, winding through the trees. They stopped here while the gates opened, then they went in. Then they went off. It was five or ten minutes after I found Robin missing. Enough time for somebody to get him out of the camper and drive him up this road."

"That would be Alvin, the director," whispered Rupert. "In his big old Cadillac."

"That's what the rangers said. Do you know him?"

"I've seen him lots of times."

"What's he look like?"

"Not good."

"What do you mean?"

"Last time I saw him was in the spring. He looked horrible. He looked like a cadaver."

"A what?"

"You asked me. He looked like death warmed over. He looked like something a dog dug up."

* * *

They waited until a cloud drifted over the moon, then walked to the gate. The bars were thick, rusted where the paint had fallen away. The old lock was bent and broken, a heavy chain and padlock in its place. Owen and Rupert looked through the bars.

An unpaved driveway led from the gate to a small round pond and turned left, disappearing in the shadows. Beyond the pond, reflected on its still, black surface, was the asylum. It was a large, two-story, Tudor building made entirely of yellow brick. Wide brick steps were set before the main entrance, where white double doors were framed by narrow leaded windows and brick columns. Thick ivy climbed the columns and covered most of the second story. Above, gables were set in a steep tiled roof. In one of them a candle burned.

"Ruthie lives up there," said Rupert. "She always burns a candle."

"What for?"

"I don't know."

Looking closely, Owen saw that every window in the asylum was heavily barred. The ivy, shining like black patent leather in the moonlight, nearly covered the entire building, creeping along the walls, up over the slate roof, and clinging in thick clumps to the tall chimneys at either end.

They could hear muffled voices, a din of human activity coming from the big house and adding to the screech of the crickets, the whine of the mosquitoes and gnats. It was late, sometime after midnight, but Mizpah sounded wide awake.

"Big, huh?" whispered Rupert.

"Is it just the one building?"

"Just the one."

"How many people in there?"

60

"About thirty, I guess. The men are on the second floor. Ruthie's got the attic. She's the only woman in the place. Can you imagine that?"

Owen looked up at the gabled window where the candle glowed.

"How many guards?"

"Three. They live on the first floor. Alvin lives in the basement."

"Alone?"

"Far as I know."

"Do the guards have cars?"

"Not likely. They're not allowed off the grounds."

"What?"

"The guards are all convicts, trusties from the state prison at Rahway. Big guys, Owen, all of them."

"Where's Alvin's car?"

"He parks it around the side. Big old Caddy convertible, shot to shit but it won't quit. Only car on the grounds."

"Does he drive much?"

"Couple times a week I see him going by. Hardly ever at night."

"How does he get his supplies?"

"Big truck comes in once a week. The state supplies him with everything."

"That's it? No visitors?"

"Hardly ever. Every once in a while you see some people drive up this road, but they never stay long."

Owen saw something moving quickly across the lawn. Grabbing Rupert's arm, he ducked behind the wall. He heard a deep growl, then loud barking. A Doberman pushed its long snout through the bars and howled, white teeth flashing in the

61

moonlight. The big dog was joined by another, snapping and snarling at the black night. The dogs had seen Owen and Rupert; now they could smell them. It was driving them wild.

"How many dogs?"

"Just those two. They're vicious, Owen. They can tear your throat right out if they want. Don't *ever* take a chance with a Doberman pinscher, specially those two. They're mad."

Owen shuddered, his eyes on the black pointed snouts, the sharp flashing teeth.

"We better move, Owen. We'll have the guards on us."

"I want a better look."

"Around the back. We can look over the wall."

"Let's go."

Owen followed Rupert along a narrow weedy path at the base of the wall. It ran straight into the woods and turned left after fifty yards. The wall was twenty feet high, made quickly and crudely from cinder block and whitewashed cement. The woods were thick with tall slender pines, oaks, willows, leatherleaf shrub, and cinnamon fern. The mosquitoes were bad.

After fifteen minutes of walking, Rupert stopped. He pointed to a tree, a giant willow, its trunk close to the wall, its branches reaching well over the top.

"You've been up there, Rupert?"

"Lots of times."

"Will it hold both of us?"

"It should."

"Okay."

Rupert began to climb. Owen followed.

When he was even with the top of the wall, Owen stopped. Hugging the smooth trunk, he looked over his shoulder at the asylum. In the distance he saw the gleaming tiled roof, still wet and glistening from the storm. He saw the chimneys, the gables, the ivy running wild in copper rain gutters, spilling over and hanging down. He kept climbing.

When he looked again the rear of the building was in full view. Spaced evenly among the thick ivy vines were barred windows, fourteen on the first floor, thirteen on the second. All of them were tall, narrow, and barred. Behind several windows on the second floor a pale light glowed. Three doors, one at either end of the building and one in the middle, were closed.

Below Owen was the top of the wall. He noted the broken bits of bottle glass set in the cement in neat rows, catching the moonlight, sparkling like stars. He climbed higher.

The tree swayed, the branches bent under his weight. Hoisting himself up the last few feet, Owen closed his eyes and held his breath until he and the tree were still. Then he looked.

Stretching away from the building was a flat wide meadow of yellow weeds broken by dark patches of what had once been lawn. There was a blighted orchard of black apple trees surrounding a ruined gazebo. A footpath meandered through the meadow, leading to a point below in the darkness by the base of the wall. Something moved on the footpath.

Owen touched Rupert's arm and pointed. A flashlight snapped on, swept the ground and went off. The moon shone through parted clouds on two figures, one taller than the other. They were walking together, coming closer.

The taller of the two was a man wearing a long

white coat. He was silver-haired and walked with a slight limp. His face was pale with dark shadows for features. He carried the flashlight, which he used to find their way along the path. They were closer now, not fifty feet from the wall, and Owen could hear the murmur of conversation.

By the man's side walked a woman. Her long rippling hair was red. Her face and hands were a powdery white that seemed to glow phosphorescently. She wore a thin white nightgown, so sheer that even from a distance Owen could see that beneath it she was naked. In her ivory white arms she carried something wrapped in a white blanket that trailed along the ground. She rocked the bundle like a baby, laughing and talking to it.

The couple arrived at a clearing at the base of the wall, just under the willow tree where Owen and Rupert were hidden. The flashlight went on, and for a moment Owen could see everything below.

The thick weeds and underbrush had been burned back, leaving a circle of sandy ground. In a neat row were several rectangular plots of trampled earth strewn with dead wild flowers. Wooden crosses, most of them rotten and broken, littered the small makeshift cemetery. The flashlight's beam traveled the ground and came to rest on a deep dark hole. The couple moved to the hole, leaned over, and looked down. It was freshly dug. Shovels and a mound of sandy earth lay nearby. It was a grave and it was empty.

At that moment the bundle in the woman's arms came alive. Owen gasped as he saw the Doberman puppy squirm and break free from her arms. The dog jumped to the ground and ran away. The woman laughed and looked back at the hole.

Chapter Four

THE MAN and the woman spoke softly, then turned back, walking arm in arm along the footpath. When they reached the asylum they entered the center doorway, and a door closed behind them with a distant thud.

"That was Ruthie," said Rupert. "The man was Dr. Alvin. Did you see him?"

"Not very well."

"You should see him. He looks terrible."

"That was my dog, Rupert, the puppy I gave my boy. He was with Robin in the camper. He was with me in the woods. How could he have gotten in there?"

"Through the bars. He could squeeze right through."

Owen nodded.

"I wonder why he would," Rupert added.

"Something's going on, Rupert. Something nobody knows about."

"Nobody really knows what goes on in there."

"I'm going to find out."

"How?"

"I'm going in."

"Oh God, Owen, don't."

"I've got to."

"Don't go in there, not alone."

"I'm going, Rupert. I've got to see if my boy's in there. I think he is."

"Then get help. Get the cops."

"The police are no help; they're against me."

"I don't mean the Troopers. I don't mean anybody from the Pines. I mean your friends, people from where you live, cops who know you."

"I don't have the time."

"Don't do it, Owen. People go in there and they don't come out."

"I'll come out."

"Please, Owen, just think about it. Anything could happen to you and nobody would know. It could swallow you up. And nobody'd ever believe me when I told them."

"I won't get swallowed up."

"You could wind up in that hole down there."

"What do you think that hole is for?"

"A body."

"Whose?"

"God knows. I don't want to find out."

"I do."

"Owen, think about it."

"I have. It's the only thing I can do. Will you help me?"

"How?"

"Wait for me by the gates. If I'm not out by dawn, go for the Troopers. Tell them to come in and get me. Okay?"

"If that's what you want."

"That's what I want. Now, how do I get in there?"

"Well, what you could do is climb onto the top of the wall and let yourself down. If you watch the glass you should be all right."

"I can do that."

66

"But, Owen, if those dogs get on you, you don't stand a chance."

"I know."

"Hear them? They're still over by the gate, barking their heads off. All they've got to do is get wind of you."

"They won't. Not if you'll help me."

"I said I would."

"Okay. Go around to the gates and let them see you. Keep them there as long as you can. It should only take me a few minutes to make it to the building."

"If they come after you, Owen, remember there's no way out."

"I know it."

"You've got nothing to defend yourself with."

"I'm okay."

"Owen, they're trained. When they attack they can't stop."

"Rupert . . . it might be crazy, but I've got to get in there right away and have a look around. If you do what I told you, I won't have any trouble with the dogs. After I get in I can handle myself."

"How do you know? How do you know there won't be things in there worse than dogs?"

"I'll handle them."

Rupert sighed. He lowered himself quickly and quietly to the ground. Owen could not see him in the darkness, but he heard his whisper.

"The Lord watch between me and thee when we are absent one from another."

"Burma Shave," whispered Owen.

"And, Owen? The door on the left . . . it's never locked."

"Thanks, Rupert."

"Don't mention it."

He heard Rupert move off through the woods. Alone, Owen began to feel sleepy, dull, weak. He shook his head and thought of Robin, the headlights, the woman, the puppy, and the hole.

Owen waited fifteen minutes then lowered himself to the top of the wall. Standing on tiptoe, clinging to a thin branch, he searched for a clear handhold among the broken glass. Suddenly the branch snapped and he lost his balance.

Owen fell the full twenty feet, landing on soft ground. As he crumpled to the earth he felt a sharp pain shoot up his right leg. Winded, his head ringing, Owen writhed in mute agony, waiting for the pain to pass. He rolled over and felt his leg. It was not broken, but his heel ached like fire when he put weight on it. Walking would be difficult, running impossible.

Taking one painful step at a time, Owen limped down the moonlit path toward the asylum.

Silver clouds raced eastward across the moon, casting ragged shadows on the big house and grounds. A warm wind came up, smelling of pine, rain, and damp earth. Owen dragged his injured heel and listened to the dogs in the distance. He was taking a long time to cross the open field.

As he neared the building, the barking stopped. Listening to the crickets, Owen peered around a corner and saw the black shape of a large automobile parked close to the building. He limped over to it for a closer look. It was a '54 Cadillac convertible, rusted, dented, and splattered with yellow pineland mud. One taillight was smashed, the hood was sprung, the top torn.

Owen opened the front door on the driver's side, and peeked in. The car reeked of dust and damp.

On the front seat was a soiled handkerchief. The glove compartment was open and empty.

He heard footsteps. Moving quickly, painfully, Owen rolled over the front seat into the rear of the car. Someone passed close by, headed for the front of the building. When Owen dared to look, he saw a fat man in a disheveled blue-and-gray uniform walking slowly away. He carried a thick nightstick, and on his belt was a holstered revolver with a double row of bullets. The guard's free hand rested on the holster.

Owen let a few minutes go by before he left the car. He was listening for the dogs when suddenly he stopped. A full-grown female Doberman was crouched in the middle of the path. The moon gleamed on the silver choke chain around its neck. Owen froze.

The dog growled. Owen extended his hand as a peace offering. The dog sprang for Owen's throat. His arm blocked the attack, but the Doberman managed to bite deeply into Owen's lower arm, twisting and tearing flesh with its razor fangs. Owen slammed the dog's head into the fender of the Cadillac and broke free.

Quickly Owen opened the rear door and jumped in. The dog was barking, jumping against the car window while Owen examined his arm. The wound was bloody, but no veins had been cut. He could see white bone, yellow sinew. Suddenly he felt sick.

A wave of nausea racked his stomach and intestines, causing him to retch violently. When he looked up, the Doberman had been joined by another. It was a male, larger, and barking more furiously than its mate. Owen backed up from the glass, fearing that the dogs might burst through. The guards would be coming at any second.

He reached for the door handle behind him, found it, and opened the door a crack. Then, leaning backward, he kicked open the other door, smashing it against the dogs. They recoiled, howling, then found their feet and leaped into the Cadillac. But by that time Owen was out the far door and on the rotting convertible top. From there he pulled both doors shut, trapping the dogs inside. He climbed quickly from the car and limped away. Behind him the dogs' furor turned to frenzy. Owen held his bloody arm close to his chest and kept moving.

Staying in the shadow of the building, Owen came to a door. He tried it, but it was locked. What was it Rupert had said? The door on the left was never locked. Owen was at the opposite end of the building. He was moving, dragging his damaged foot, when he saw the big guard coming.

Owen stepped into the dark center doorway before the guard could see him. He flattened himself against the door and held his breath. The guard passed close by, so close that Owen could smell him. The hulking form moved onward toward the Cadillac and disappeared around the corner of the building. Owen tried the door, but it was locked.

He could hear the dogs scrambling for freedom just as he reached the far door. It was slightly ajar and swung open easily and quietly. Owen slipped through and tried to close the door behind him, but the lock had fallen off or been torn away. He paused to let his eyes adjust to the darkness. He was in a stairwell with iron steps leading up and down to darkness.

The odor inside the building was overpowering.

The stairwell reeked of excrement, urine, chemical pine-scent, and ammonia. Owen's head reeled. He shook it, flinging from him the dizziness, nausea, fear, and disgust he felt for the fetid atmosphere.

He decided to try the basement. At the bottom of the stairs he was stopped by a steel door with a keyhole but no handle. The door was locked. Owen felt his way back to the ground floor, climbed a dozen steps and found a heavy oaken door. When he turned its iron handle, the door swung open.

He was in a wide corridor with white walls and ceiling and a black-and-white checkerboard floor. The linoleum was highly polished and smelled of wax. The walls were spotless and bare. The corridor ran the length of the building and was lighted by a single fluorescent fixture in the center, just above the building's main entrance. White doors lined both sides of the hallway and several of them were partially open.

Owen could hear snoring close by. He could hear the dogs outside, yapping and snarling, running around the building. But loudest of all was the din from the floor above, a racket that rose and fell like heavy waves landing on a rocky shore. Kicking off his muddy shoes, he crept quietly down the hall.

Peeking through an open door, he saw the dim figure of a man asleep on a cot, snoring softly. The room was cell-like and bare, white from floor to ceiling. There was a washstand, a chair, and one barred window. On the chair was a cast-off uniform, blue and gray. On the washstand was a set of keys.

Owen was in the room, on the keys, and back out again in a few seconds. Feeling their cool, jagged surfaces in his palm, he stopped to think.

Robin was still alive; he had to be. He was somewhere in this building, asleep, drugged, or awake and very frightened. He had been brought here by car, and the car belonged to the director. Alvin lived in the basement, alone, Rupert had said. Owen turned back to the door by which he had entered.

No key fit the lock in the steel door to the basement quarters. Behind it he could hear nothing, absolute silence. He returned to the long corridor and tried every door. One room was an office, sterile and drab. On a gray steel desk was a telephone. Owen tried it; the line was dead. Another room served as a waiting room, but looked as if it were never used. At the far end of the hall were double doors, steel and firmly locked.

Owen opened them with the third key he tried. Beyond was a stairwell with wide wooden steps leading upward to the second floor. The clamor from above was louder now. He climbed cautiously, listening to his heart beat. Somewhere below him, in the corridor, a door slammed. From somewhere above came a hoarse scream followed by laughter.

Two doors, set with large glass panes, opened on the second-floor landing. Beyond them was a room lit by one bare bulb, a yellow brown incandescence in the center of the ceiling. Under its murky glow was a guard fast asleep on a wooden bench. Beyond him were paned doors like the first, except that a nightstick had been thrust through their handles, barring them. Owen took a deep breath and slipped into the room, his eyes on the sleeping guard.

Set into the walls, three to a side, were six steel

72

doors. In each door was a small trapdoor on a
hinge. The trapdoors were closed, but in each of
them was a glass-lensed peephole. Owen closed
one eye and looked in a peephole.

He saw a narrow cell with padded floor and
walls. In the center of the floor, down on all fours,
was a naked black man. He was thin and muscular, wide awake, and staring at the peephole. He
reminded Owen of the Doberman outside, except
his eyes were even more animal, more savage.
Owen moved away.

In the next two rooms men slept naked on the
canvas-covered floors. The other three cubicles
were empty. All the noise was coming from beyond the barred double doors. Owen slipped the
nightstick from the handles, opened the doors,
and passed inside. He looked back and saw the
guard still sleeping, his head thrown back.

Turning, Owen came face to face with a small,
monkey-faced, old man in soiled pajamas.

"Hi ya, buddy," said the little man. "You here
for the funeral?"

Over the old man's shoulder, at the end of a long
row of cots, Owen saw a television set mounted
high on a wall. On the big screen a white-suited
evangelist was attempting to restore sight to a
woman blinded by lightning fifty years before.
His voice trembled when he spoke, and was answered by a throng of men who sat on cots or the
floor close to the set.

"Do you believe on His name?" yelled the minister, holding a white Bible over his head.

The old woman looked sightlessly into the camera, clasped her hands, and cried, "I believe on the
holy name of the Savior, *Jesus Christ!*"

"Jesus Christ," echoed the men, repeating it

like a chant, rising and clapping their hands, dancing around the set.

"Did you bring us a body?" whispered the old man to Owen.

Ignoring him, Owen scanned the large room. Metal lockers lined the walls, a cot in front of each locker. The walls were painted dark green halfway to the ceiling, where they changed to a light green. On several cots men slept or lay quietly, sheetless, in cotton pajamas. The dormitory smelled of sickness and sweat. The noise was constant.

"Do you love *Jesus?*" screamed the minister.

"Jesus, Jesus, Jesus!" shrieked the men.

"We need a body," said the old man, looking at Owen from head to toe.

"Sorry," said Owen, "I just got here."

"Where from?"

"State hospital."

The old, monkey-faced man sat on a cot and patted the canvas beside him.

"Have a seat?"

Owen sat with his back to the far end of the room. Apart from the old man no one had seen him. If he could get some information, he could leave without disturbing the men, who might call the guard.

"When's the funeral?"

"In the morning," said the old man, slapping his knee. "You coming?"

"Who's going?"

"Everybody. The boys and the vegetables."

"Vegetables?"

The old man's arm swung out, indicating the group behind him. "Most of them is vegetables. No mind at all."

"Do you believe on the power?" blared the television.

"I believe!" shouted the inmates.

"Do you believe on heaven and hell?"

"Heaven and hell!"

"Have you seen a little boy in here?" asked Owen. "A little boy only this high?" He held out his hand.

The old man shook his head, picked his nose.

"Have you seen the director tonight?"

"Dr. Alvin? Not tonight. You won't see him tonight."

"Why not?"

"He don't like our funerals. He makes himself scarce."

"Whose funeral is it?"

"God only knows. We don't even have a body yet."

"Heaven and hell and sin and lust!" bawled the minister.

"Lust!" bellowed the inmates. *"Sin and lust!"*

"I don't get it," said Owen.

"Because you're new."

"I'm new."

"Welcome to Mizpah," said the old man. He giggled, looked around the room and back at Owen. "We got good funerals here. Great ones."

"Tell me about them."

"One time a month. We all get together for a nice Christian ceremony. Then we bury somebody. Ha!"

"Where, out back?"

"Right out back in the cemetery. Plenty of people down there, fella. Some nights you can hear them digging and scraping, trying to get out of their boxes, out of their holes!"

"Will you walk a little closer to the Lord?" thundered the minister.

"Oh, Lord!" screamed the inmates. *"Lord, Lord, Lord! Oh, Lord, God help us!"*

Owen looked closely at the old man. His head was small and bald, his back bent. His right knee trembled violently. His wrinkled, flesh-colored pajamas had short arms and legs and were torn at the seams. The toenails of his bare feet were black. Around his neck a soiled gauze bandage was tied like a scarf. His toothless mouth worked constantly, whether he was speaking or not. He made Owen think of his father.

"Have you been here long?" he asked.

"Years. And don't ask me how many."

"Who put you here?"

"You got a minute? I'll tell you."

"Go ahead."

"I was a sergeant in the army, in the Pacific. I got captured by the enemy. Spent four years in a prison camp. When I got out I had to spend a year in a veteran's hospital to get over what they did in the prison camp. Then the doctors let me out, said I was okay." The old man grabbed his knee to make it stop shaking. He became quiet.

"Well, see, when I shipped out I was a married man. Just married a couple months when I had to go. Five years went by and I'm back. I come home and my wife's got a baby, two years old."

"Oh."

"She was alone with the baby, living off my benefits. Right in my hometown, Paterson. I come home a war hero and I can't show my face in Paterson, see?"

Owen nodded.

"She begged me to forgive her. She said she was

76

lonely all those years. Said the man just happened to be around, that's all. Turns out he was one of my best friends. Punctured eardrum. Didn't have to go!"

"Go on."

"I went out to a bar and thought about it. I got a load on and I made my decision. I went home and told her I'd forgive her. But we couldn't live in Paterson, could we?"

"I guess not."

"We packed everything we had and by that night we were on the train. Going to live in Philadelphia. Start all over again. New city, new life. Was that good?"

"Sure," said Owen.

"We get halfway to Philly and she starts crying. I ask her what's the matter and she gets up and goes to the bathroom with the baby. I wait and I wait but she didn't come back. I go up and knock on the door. She comes out with the kid. She's still crying. We go out and stand between the cars so's we can have it out. I ask her what's the matter. She can't stop crying to talk. Finally she tells me she can't go to Philly. I ask her why not. She says she's got to go back to Paterson. She's got to be near the man. The baby's father. My best friend. And she can't even live with him because he's married. But she's got to go back to him, that's all."

"What happened?"

"I pushed them off the train. Both of them."

"Both . . ."

"Pretty bad, huh?"

"I guess so."

"Evil," said the old man.

"You were pretty upset," Owen offered.

77

"Upset? I was *nuts!*"

"You had to be."

"But at least I had a reason." The old man chuckled. "There's boys back there that are bad, and there's those who are evil. But most of them go beyond evil. They don't have any reason at all for things they do."

"Do you think you'll ever get out?"

"I doubt it."

"Why not? I don't think you're crazy now."

"You don't?"

"No."

The old man crossed his eyes, stuck out his tongue, and slapped Owen across the face.

"Fink!" shouted Monkey-face. He stood on the cot, pointed at Owen, and shouted, "Fink!"

The inmates were watching a toothpaste commercial when the old man shouted. They turned, saw Owen, and began babbling.

The old man grabbed Owen's wrist, shouted in his ear, "Judas!" The inmates came running.

Twisting away, Owen dashed for the double doors. He ran into the outstretched arms of a short fat man whose head and part of his face were wrapped in bandages. Hugged hard against the short, stocky body, Owen was lifted from the ground. He looked down into an idiot's face, contorted, ageless, gaping, and slobbering. Green teeth clenched a purple tongue. Purple lips opened and sang in a ghastly wail:

Dance with the dolly with the
    hole in her stocking, hole in her stocking,
    hole in her stocking.
Dance with the dolly with the
    hole in her stocking,

78

Dance by the light of the moon!

The fat man dropped Owen and began to dance. Hopping on one foot and holding the other, he performed a macabre jig on the polished linoleum. The other inmates moved in on Owen, but he scrambled away and ran for the doors.

He was almost there when he slipped and fell. Getting up, he saw a dozen fast-moving forms in gray pajamas, running toward him from all sides. Jabbering like jackasses, they closed in.

He screamed once before a cold hand clamped over his mouth. He was wrestled to the ground, his limbs pinned by the frantic mob. He was powerless. He felt their hands moving over him, feeling his body through his clothes, unbuttoning his shirt and his pants. He saw their grinning, maniacal faces, their shaggy, matted hair, their filthy hands. Saliva drooled from their gaping mouths as they shrieked and babbled above him. Their eager eyes fastened on his crotch and widened when his underwear was torn away.

One of the men cracked his teeth together like dice. Another bellowed like a bull, his head thrown back, tongue hanging out, tears on his cheeks.

Then Owen saw the knife.

Six men held him down. Six men spread his legs apart. The one with the knife, a tall thin man with big ears and a bulbous nose, long greasy hair and a full black beard, came between them. He held the knife carefully in his right hand. With his left thumb he tested the edge. The knife was crude, made from blackened steel.

Owen tried to scream, but the cold hand clamped down harder.

"Fink!" someone screamed.

"Judas!"

"Twist his nose, twist his toes!"

"Spit on him!"

"Smear him!"

"Cut it, Cebulski!" shouted the old man. "Cut it right off!"

"Dance with the dolly, dance with the dolly, dance, dance, *dance!*"

". . . and he walked," droned the minister, "and he talked, and he said to the man of Bethlehem . . ."

"*Dance!*"

The knife came closer, waving in the air over Owen's exposed crotch. Owen heaved with all his might, but men were sitting on his arms and legs, and he could not throw them off.

"Kill the freak!"

"Catch his blood!"

". . . took bread and blessed it and gave it to the disciples, and said eat this, for this is my body . . ."

"Bite him!"

"Eat him!"

"Dance by the light of the *moon!*"

". . . drink ye all of it for this is my blood . . ."

"Suck him! Suck his blood!"

"Make him *dance!*"

Suddenly bright lights snapped on. Instantly the knife disappeared. The inmates howled as a guard came crashing into their midst. Swinging his long black club, he drove the men before him like frightened cattle. Owen rolled under a cot, hoping he hadn't been seen.

Looking for his clothes, he found a set of gray pajamas, soiled and reeking, but they fit. He remained hidden while the guard screamed at the hysterical men gathered at the far end of the room, cringing below the blaring television set.

The guard was tall and heavyset. His arms were tanned and muscular, his shoulders wide. He smashed a steel locker with his club, silencing the babble.

"When're you fuckin' animals going to get some sleep, huh? When're you gonna let *me* get some sleep, huh?" He was hoarse, as if he'd been shouting all day.

"Okay, Patsy," they said. "Okay, okay." Some of them edged toward cots. He waved them back with his club.

"Who started the fight?" he demanded.

"Was no fight," said Monkey-face.

"Shut up, Patruzi," said the guard. "Who started it?"

"It's over, Patsy," said the bearded man who had held the knife. "No trouble."

"What were you up to, Cebulski?"

"We were celebrating."

"Celebrating what?"

"The beauty of the Word."

"Amen," said an inmate. "Amen," repeated the others. They were smiling now. It seemed to Owen that they were playing along, enjoying a grand game that could last forever. "Oh, the beauty," they said.

"We were filled with the Glory!"

"Oh, the Glory!" wailed a young man with sores on his face. "Oh, Christ's Glory."

"I am a wicked, wicked woman," said the blind woman on television, her gaze slightly off camera.

"Sinner!" shouted the faith healer.

Furious, the guard kicked a cot across the room.

"Remember this: you freaks give me any more trouble and we call off the funeral!"

Two men burst into tears.

A pale-faced man with a potbelly shrieked and tore at his hair. The man next to him bellowed, honked.

Cebulski, the bearded knife-wielder, stammered in rage, choked on his tongue, clawed his face.

Owen was waiting for a chance to escape when he saw the double doors open. Through them came a tall, white-haired man in a white coat. Owen had seen him earlier. In the graveyard with the girl.

"Doctor, doctor!" wailed old Patruzi. "He's calling off the funeral!"

"I didn't say that!" shouted the guard.

"He did, he did!" cried Cebulski.

"No funeral!" screamed the men.

"Nonsense," said the director. "The funeral will be held as planned." His voice was low and calm. Owen, lying on the floor twenty feet away, looked at him in the flickering light from the television set.

The director's eyes were magnified by a pair of round, steel-rimmed spectacles. His skin was sallow, stretched like parchment over sunken cheeks. He walked with a limp, holding his right hand stiffly to his side. Despite his white hair and his spotted sickly skin, Alvin looked aged but not old. His appearance did not match his voice, which was that of a younger man.

"Mr. Mahoney," he said to the guard, "return to your post, please."

The guard backed away from the inmates, turned, and walked through the double doors.

"We're gonna have the funeral?" someone shouted.

"Yes, of course. Preparations have begun."

"Have we got a body?" someone asked politely.

"I believe so."

"I believe!" someone declared.

"I believe on His name!" cried the blind woman, whose sight was now restored.

"God's love, oh God!" yelled the minister.

"God, God, God, God, God, God, God, God!" shouted everyone.

"I think it's time we turned off the television and went to sleep," said Dr. Alvin.

"No, no, no!" said Cebulski.

"I want to sleep," said the young man with sores.

"Get fucked," said the man next to him.

"Gentlemen," said the director, "it's well after midnight. Some of us want to sleep, some would like to go on watching. Suppose we turn off the sound? Mr. Sprouter, would you kindly turn off the sound?"

A Negro, taller than the rest, stretched and turned a knob that was just within his reach. The set was silent.

"Thank you," said the director, turning to go.

"But we can't hear the Word," said Cebulski.

Alvin looked at the bearded man, smiled, and said nothing.

"How can we hear the Word?"

"You can't, Mr. Cebulski," said the director.

"You can't do that," said Cebulski evenly.

"No?"

"You can't keep us from the Word."

"Are you going to behave, Mr. Cebulski?"

83

asked the director, "or are you going to be . . ." He paused for effect. ". . . bad?"

The word jolted the room.

Cebulski sat on a cot and wrung his hands. "I'm gonna be good," he said.

"I knew you would," said Alvin, smiling.

"He's gonna be good, doctor," said old Patruzi, his monkey-face gone limp.

"*I'm* good," said the young man.

"*I'm* good," said someone else, giggling.

"Good," said the doctor.

"We're all good," said a fat man with freckles.

"I hope so," said the director, "because we know that one bad apple . . . one *bad* apple . . . can spoil the barrel."

"Oh no!" somebody said.

"He's *bad!*" somebody shouted. "Get him out!"

"Who?" asked the director.

"Cebulski," said someone from a dark corner. "He's got a knife."

The director held out his hand, looked at Cebulski. "Give it here," he said.

"I don't have no knife."

"Yes he does."

"Give it here, Mr. Cebulski."

Cebulski shook his head.

Four men pounced on him, threw him to the floor.

The scuffle ended quickly. The tall Negro approached Alvin and handed him the makeshift knife, handle first. Alvin looked at it, weighing it in his hand.

"Now, this is bad," he said.

"*Bad!*" someone screamed.

"Cebulski's *bad!*"

"He's the *bad* apple, doctor!"

"Put him out, put him out!"

"Put him in the *Bad Room,*" hollered Patruzi.

"Oh, sweet Jesus!" someone shouted. "The *Bad Room!*"

"Gentlemen," said the doctor, regarding the knife and then Cebulski, "this is as *bad* as it gets."

"Get him out, doctor."

"Burn him."

"Bury him!"

"Put him in the *Bad Room!*"

Cebulski, borne down the aisle by five men, offered no resistance. The guard opened the door and held it open.

"You want him in the *Bad Room,* doctor?" he asked.

Alvin paused. Everyone waited.

"Isolation," he said, nodding his head toward the vestibule. "I'm very busy tonight."

"Thank you, doctor," said Cebulski on his way by.

"We'll talk tomorrow, Mr. Cebulski. I'm very disappointed."

"I'm not *bad,*" he screamed just before they closed the door.

The director looked back at the silent ward. The men were settling onto their cots, pulling sheets over themselves, pounding pillows into shape.

"Sleep well, gentlemen," said Alvin.

"Funeral tomorrow?" whispered Patruzi.

"In the morning," Alvin replied kindly.

"You gonna get us a body?"

Alvin chuckled. "We'll see." The guard opened the double doors and the white-haired man limped out.

Owen waited until he heard loud snoring, then

began to move about, searching for the set of keys, which had fallen from his hand. Squirming on his stomach, sliding across the polished linoleum, he found them under an empty locker. Raising his head above the level of the cots, he looked around.

The ward was half empty. The men lay on the cots closest to the television set, at the other end of the room from Owen. When he was sure they were all asleep he tiptoed to the double doors. The billy club was thrust through the handles, the guard asleep on the wooden bench, as before. Owen looked for another exit.

On his right was a narrow door, unmarked and firmly locked. Owen found the key, opened the door and stepped through. He was in a long narrow kitchen, a room of cabinets and counters, a large refrigerator, and two stoves. The walls were a pale yellow and were greasy to the touch. Moonlight shone through two barred windows, and through them Owen could see stars, the black Pine Barrens, the high white wall.

His bruised heel still bothered him, but it was his wounded arm that worried Owen. Turning on a faucet, he let a stream of warm water pour over the lacerated flesh. He passed a bar of strong-smelling kitchen soap over the torn skin and winced as searing pain shot up his arm. He found a dry rag and wound it around his arm, tore it, and tied it off. His heart was pounding and his head ached.

Suddenly he felt dizzy, weak, about to faint. He slapped his face, leaning against the wall until the feeling passed. His brain and his body were trying to close down, find rest, sleep. But Owen said no.

At the far end of the room was another door. Unlocking it, he saw a narrow stairway leading down to the first floor. At the bottom of the steps a door opened at the turn of a glass knob. He was back in the long white corridor with the white doors, the white light, and the checkerboard floor.

Clutching his keys, Owen limped to the stairway he had entered by, and went down the steps in the darkness. Once outside he paused to breathe the fresh air, so sweet and clean after the acrid, sour, sick smell of the institution. Again a blackness came over him, a shutting down of consciousness, an escape to the limbo of shock. Owen fought it, refused to surrender, admit defeat. His head cleared at the sound of dogs barking. In a moment he was on his way.

The heavy oaken door that Alvin and Ruth Sooey had taken opened with a brass key. A circular iron staircase wound upward through a dimly lit shaft. Barred windows with broken panes admitted moonlight, showed the rusty steps, the cracks and gaps in the old plaster. At the first floor was a landing with a door, then the steps spiraled without interruption to the attic. Owen stopped before a steel door with a keyhole, no handle.

Putting his ear to the door, he heard music playing softly. In the darkness he tried every key he had, but none would fit. He knocked lightly.

A woman's voice answered.

"Rupert?"

Chapter Five

RUPERT?

Owen put an eye to the keyhole and looked in. He saw a large room lighted by many candles, a huge four-poster bed, and a woman taking a bath in a long zinc tub. She had stopped her washing and was looking at the door. He knocked again softly, his eye on her.

"Rupert, is that you?" she asked again.

Owen whispered yes through the keyhole. She got out of the tub, her blazing red hair clinging to moon white shoulders. Owen straightened as the door opened. She stood before him, smiling and expectant. When she saw his face she stopped smiling.

"I'm Rupert's friend," Owen blurted out. "He's right outside at the gate—"

Ruth's knee shot up, catching Owen hard in the crotch. He bent double, but did not cry out. As he crumpled to the floor she clipped him behind the ear with both fists. Owen saw stars, felt the light fading, but hung on. On his side, clutching his aching groin, he watched Ruth walk calmly across the room and pick up a softball bat. She returned and stood over him, bathwater dripping from her body to his face.

"You want to wind up in the Bad Room?" she asked.

Owen gasped, "Rupert Sooey's my friend. I know your mother, Rose Sooey. She used to have a dog named Dee. Your father made moonshine."

Ruth let out a whimper and dropped the bat. She knelt beside Owen and looked in his face. "Who the hell are you?"

"Help me," said Owen, trying to rise.

She got him to his feet and walked him to a large overstuffed chair. Owen sat down, his legs spread, his hands resting protectively over his battered groin. Without bothering to cover herself, Ruth went away and returned with a glass of water, which she held to his lips while he drank. The water was rusty and tasted of earth.

"My name is Owen Vanderbes," he said, trying to calm himself. "I'm sorry I scared you."

Ruth looked at him critically. "When were you admitted?"

Owen looked down at himself. The pajamas he wore were soiled and shredded. He was barefoot, his skin smeared with mud and blood. He looked worse than the poor wretches in the dormitory below.

He shook his head. "I wasn't admitted. I'm not a patient. I sneaked in."

Ruth laughed, raised a red eyebrow. "You sneaked into Mizpah? How?"

"Over the wall. Your brother showed me."

Ruth blinked her large green eyes. "Why?"

Owen began to tell her everything he had seen, heard, and done that night. The story was long, and while he told it Ruth settled back into the bathtub and continued her bath. She listened carefully with only her eyes showing over the rim.

When he was finished she stared at the ceiling, deep in thought. Owen waited for her reaction.

"And you think Alvin might have taken your baby boy," she said softly.

"Do you think it's possible?"

Ruth stood and stepped out of the tub. Candle-light played on her naked flesh as she slowly dried herself with a threadbare towel.

"It's possible," she said when she was dry. "Anything's possible these days."

She walked behind a painted screen, Chinese landscape on tattered silk. Music, a waltz, began to play under a scratchy needle.

"Will you help me find him?" Owen asked.

There was no answer. He could hear her opening and closing drawers, changing the record. While she dressed, Owen examined the room.

The long low attic chamber had windows set in gables on both sides of the steeply sloping roof. The walls were papered with faded hunting scenes, green and white. Books were piled everywhere, stacked in corners, spilling from bookshelves, crammed under tables and chairs. The antique Victorian furniture was worn, unmended. A vanity with a cracked mirror stood by a door on the far wall. In one gable was a kitchenette, a huge pot boiling bathwater on a gas stove. There were two more chairs like the one Owen sat in. In the middle of the room, resting on a low platform, was the bed.

The old four-poster had a canopy of lace, torn and yellowed with age. The lace bedspread was frayed and needed washing. The sheets and pillowcases were white silk, old and rusted, wrinkled and stained. The bed was unmade, a swirl of bone white linen and shredded lace.

"Want a drink?" Ruth asked from behind the screen.

"I'm okay," said Owen.

Ruth, wearing a clean terrycloth bathrobe and a towel around her head, walked to the bed and sat down. She was short and thin, and in the big bed she looked like a child. In one hand she held a glass, in the other a bottle of gin. She poured herself a drink, sipped it and said, "Alvin's sick. He doesn't always know what he's doing."

"I don't understand."

"Mizpah did it to him. Mizpah burnt him out."

"You mean working with sick people made him sick?"

"*Living* with sick people. This is the only home he's ever had. How do you like it?"

"I don't like it."

"Mizpah has a disease. It was diseased when it was built and it's gotten worse over the years, like all of us. Alvin caught the disease." She smiled, raised her glass to Owen. "So did I." She drank.

"Where is he?"

"He lives in the basement."

"Thank you, Ruth." Owen stood, started for the door.

"I wouldn't run on down there if I were you," she said.

"Why not?"

"If I were you I wouldn't go near him till I knew what I was up against."

Owen returned to the bed, sat beside her. "What are you saying, Ruth?"

"I'm just saying . . . that if you knew what I know . . . you wouldn't go running on down there. Not just yet."

"Tell me," said Owen. "Tell me what you know."

Ruth's eyes widened. She looked at an open window where a candle burned, listening. "You hear it?" she asked.

"What?" Owen heard nothing.

"Barn owl."

"Tell me about Alvin, Ruth. Please?"

"Do you trust me, Owen?"

"Well . . . yes."

"Do you think I'm sick?"

"I don't know. I don't think so."

"Why not?"

"If you were crazy I'd see it in your eyes."

"You could be fooled. Anybody can be tricked."

"Not me."

"Look at me."

Ruth stared into Owen's eyes. Owen, unblinking, stared back. Ruth's eyes were large, green, flecked with gold. They were clear and bright, cat's eyes, unshifting. Owen's were brown, red-rimmed and bloodshot. They were pleading, anxious, desperate.

"What do you see, Owen?"

"Trouble."

"Disease?"

"No. Just problems, worry, frustration."

"You can tell all that from a person's eyes?"

"Anybody can."

Ruth held an antique hand-mirror to her face, studied her eyes. She stared for several minutes, then put the mirror down. In the corner of her right eye was a tear. She brushed it away and looked at Owen.

"I'll help you. I'll do whatever I can."

"Tell me about Alvin. Tell me everything."

"I've known Alvin since I was a kid," she said, pouring another inch of gin. "Did Rupert tell you?"

Owen shook his head. Was the pounding he heard his heart, or someone on the stairs?

"I had one hell of a childhood, Owen. I mean, by any standards at all, my youth was shit. It's something I never think about or talk about, but I've got to tell you a few things so you'll understand, okay?"

"Tell me." The beating was his heart, but there were other sounds, creakings and groanings behind the walls, beneath his feet.

"I'm going to be frank, Owen. Can I be frank with you?"

"Sure."

"My mother's a drunk and always has been. My father was drunk and crazy. He started sleeping with me when I was eleven."

She stared at Owen for his reaction. Owen nodded blankly and she continued.

"I grew up fast. Dusty had me working the bar since I could walk. I didn't go to school much. My school was a bar, bottles, and drunks. Dusty should be shot for doing that to me. It's too late to shoot my daddy.

"I was cute and pretty and the men liked me. I knew everybody in the Pines—the men that is. No woman would ever go in Sooey's Bar, not in those days. Dusty ran the place very loosely, and a lot went on in there that was definitely un-Christian, if you know what I mean."

Again Owen nodded, recalling the gloomy interior of the bar on Zion Road.

"All the men wanted me and they were waiting. Waiting for me to get old enough. My father didn't wait. Can you imagine that, Owen? He couldn't wait for God or nature. One night when Dusty was dead drunk he got me."

She took another drink and lay back on her bed. Raising her knees, she showed her bare legs through the opening of her bathrobe. She stared at the tattered canopy and chose her words carefully.

"I don't remember what it was like, just that he'd done it. I knew what he'd done and I was a little scared. He told me there was nothing to worry about. He said anything that felt that good couldn't be bad. He was my own father. I was eleven years old, Owen."

Owen lowered his eyes, shook his head.

"He started doing it a lot. Once or twice a week, when he got drunk enough. The other nights he slept with Dusty or some other woman. When I was twelve I reached puberty. I started to get jealous. I wanted him to myself. I liked it, Owen. By the time I was twelve, thirteen, I liked it a lot. It was wrong, maybe, but it wasn't *bad.*"

There was a scuffling sound at the door.

Owen jumped. "What's that?"

Ruth laughed. "Rats."

"Are you sure?" The noise came again.

"They come up from the basement. It's full of them." She picked up a worn slipper and flung it at the door. The noise stopped. "Where was I?"

"Talking about your father."

"I was?"

"You said you were jealous."

"Me, jealous? Never. I knew what he was doing with other women. I used to watch. It was he who got jealous when I started doing it with other men. I was about fourteen then, still working in Sooey's, no pay. I had all the men I wanted, and pretty soon they were fighting over me. I didn't care who I was doing it with. Then, one night, Alvin came in.

"He was good-looking then. Tall, black hair, sensitive eyes. He talked like no man I'd ever met. He wasn't a Piney or a Trooper or a truck driver or a farmer. He was a doctor. He started talking to *me*.

"I wasn't shy. I grew up in a bar and got over that fast. I could talk to anybody about anything, and Alvin was a good talker. He was a charmer then, at least he seemed that way to me, fourteen years old."

Ruth lit a cigarette. For a moment she was lost in her memories, nervously puffing smoke and studying her hands. Her eyes fell on Owen. "Should I stop?"

"No. Please go on. I want to know about Alvin."

They both heard the footsteps moving slowly up the stairs. Owen sprang up, retreating to the farthest corner of the room. Ruth was still, waiting, staring at the door. The footsteps paused outside. There was no knock.

"Who's there?" Ruth demanded.

"Me," said a strange voice.

Owen picked up the softball bat. Ruth waved a finger at him.

"Welter?" she asked calmly.

"Yes, miss. Is there anything you want?"

"No, Welter. Just go away."

"Can I just stand here?"

"Welter, are you looking at me through the keyhole?"

"Yes, miss."

Ruth walked to the door, looked through the

95

keyhole. "Welter, you know what I'm going to do next time I catch you?"

"No, ma'am."

"I'm going to jam my ice pick right in your eye."

"I won't . . . I'm sorry, Miss Ruth."

"Welter, get the fuck away from my door, hear?"

The footsteps retreated down the stairs. Owen tiptoed to the bed. "You think he saw me?"

"Didn't sound like it. If he did he wouldn't rat on me. Don't mind Welter, it's not his fault. I used to let him watch all he wanted."

"Is he a guard?"

"No, he's a nut. Shame the way Alvin lets him run around loose."

"Ruth," Owen pleaded, "there's not much time. Tell me about Alvin."

"He walked into Sooey's one night during a storm. It was winter and the place was packed. He got to talking to me, and he talked like I was a woman, which I *was*. I knew he ran this place and I asked him about it. He said he loved it here. Said his work was fascinating, challenging, rewarding. He had big plans for Mizpah and later on he told me all about them."

She exhaled blue smoke toward the canopy. "They were only dreams, but they were his dreams and when he talked to me about them I felt important. We made love that night in the backseat of his old Cadillac, same one he has now."

"Ruth, did he use that car tonight, just before the storm?"

"I don't know. I was asleep. Christ, I had the wildest dreams tonight. Owen, are you interested in other people's dreams?"

"Well, not right now. Right now I'm interested in the man who runs this place."

"He was the first man who ever took his time with me. I thought that when a man and a woman made love, the woman just laid there open. I thought men had to be rough and tough to get what they wanted. Alvin was tender and good. It woke me up. I changed. I stopped taking shit off of every man I screwed. But I only got in more and more trouble."

She stubbed out her cigarette and lit another. Owen waited patiently for her to continue.

"I had troubles, Owen. Whatever happened, it was always my fault. I'd sleep with a man and the man would go home and beat up his wife. It happens. Then, next day, the poor wife would tell the minister and the minister would tell her it was Ruth Sooey's fault. Or fights would start between two men. Over me. I had a father and his own son fighting over me.

"The women were terrible. They'd spit on me when they saw me. They'd scream things as I went by. I had to stay away from school, away from the towns. I couldn't go to the store but somebody'd come up to me with a bad situation that was my fault.

"But it was the men who hurt me the most. I had a boyfriend. He was married and had kids, but he said he was getting a divorce. I was going out with lots of men then, but he told me I was his alone. I was fifteen, he was forty-five, strong as a horse. He caught me with another guy. It was at a drive-in movie in Cardif. He beat up the other guy and put him in the hospital. Then he drove me over to his house and tied me to a tree in the backyard and he whipped me with a clothesline. His

97

kids were asleep, but his wife wasn't. She stood on the porch and laughed. When he got tired she came down and whipped me. She didn't get tired for a long time."

Ruth took a drink and stared at the canopy.

"Once I was walking down Zion Road. The Troopers pulled up and told me to get in the back. They didn't say where we were going. They drove me up to a town called Og's Hat, over in the next county. They took me to a farm and called the farmer out. He came out with his wife and they both looked at me. They said no, I wasn't the girl they were looking for. So we turned around and drove back. But on the way they stopped. Drove the car up a dirt road and told me I had to blow both of them or they'd arrest me for prostitution. They said the judge would send me straight to Bordentown—reform school. I was always being threatened with Bordentown. I'm fifteen and I had to blow both those State Troopers on the hood of the squad car. And they knew they'd get away with it because of my reputation. I had the worst reputation in the history of the Pines, I can tell you. I went to church once, just once, to see somebody get married, and the minister told me to get out.

"The only person who was nice to me was Alvin. He understood me and he made no demands. When we could get together we would. If I didn't see him for a while that was okay, too. And it wasn't all sex between us, like the others. We talked a lot, mostly about this place, his patients. We talked about mental disease and mental health. He had a lot of theories he'd thought up himself. He's a trained psychologist, you know."

"He's not a medical doctor?"

"No. He's got a Ph.D. in psychology. He's a genius, Owen, I'm sure of that. At least he was then. He could talk for hours and I wouldn't understand a word. But I was a good listener just the same. We were lovers, sure, but we were also great friends. He told me once that if I got into a jam he'd help me out. I was seventeen when I got into a big jam.

"My father was drinking more than ever. It was a race between him and Dusty to see who could stay drunkest the longest. I wouldn't sleep with him and he got jealous. He knew all about my activities. He didn't care what I did as long as I did it with him when he wanted me. But I stopped doing it with him and he got mad. He told Dusty.

"Dusty and I had had some fights in our time. But this one was a real battle. Dusty loves a battle, especially if it's in front of other people. The bar was half full when she started on me. Called me every name in the book while the men laughed. I'll never forget that night. I was looking at the men. I'd been friends with most of them, and I'd slept with a lot of them. But the way they were laughing and looking at me I knew they hated me. They hated me because they figured I was *bad.*"

She paused, looked at Owen, and laughed. "I wasn't bad. I was good. I liked anybody who liked me. And I was the best screw in the Pines."

"Go on."

"Dusty was saying terrible things, things I won't repeat even after ten years. My own mother. I was yelling back at her, saying a few things myself. I knew that she slept with other men every once in a while. I mentioned that. She went crazy. She threw a bottle at me. Told me to get out and

99

never come back. It was her bar, her house. I had
to do what she said. I moved out.

"I didn't have a dime. There was no place I
wanted to go. So I went into the woods. I picked a
nice old car in there and I moved in. I lived in the
car all summer. I picked cranberries, strawber-
ries, peaches, everything, anything to make a
little money. I didn't tell anybody where I lived
because I was scared living in the woods all alone.
But I missed men.

"I met a man in Buena. He had a chicken farm
and he wasn't married. He was a lot older than I,
but I always liked older men. He got me to tell him
where I was living. Then he started to visit me. It
was kind of scary because we were way out there
in the woods and I really didn't know him that
well. I was thinking about moving to another part
of the Pines when he showed up one night with a
friend. They were both drunk.

"He screwed me in front of the other man. Then
he made way for the other man. But I wasn't
going to be treated like that. I got away and I hid
in the woods. I heard a lot of yelling and then it
got quiet. I came back for a look. There he was, the
chicken farmer, sitting against a tree. He was all
bloody and there was a knife stuck in his stomach.
I tried to help him, to comfort him as best I could.
But he died in about fifteen minutes.

"In the morning I got to a phone first thing. The
Troopers met me and I took them in the woods and
showed them. They took me back with them to the
barracks and charged me with murder. They said
I'd done it and was lying about the other guy.
They said there was no other guy. They worked on
me, Owen, but I stuck to my story.

"I was locked up at the Cape May County Court

House with no lawyer, no money, nothing. I didn't think I had a chance. I didn't think I'd ever get out of there. And one day, all of a sudden, they said I could go. Dr. Alvin had paid my bail.

"He got me to a lawyer and we talked the whole thing over. They said everything was against me. They said the State was getting ready to nail me for life. The only chance I had was to plead temporary insanity. They made up a story about the man beating me, going after me with the knife. I had to agree to it, I had to tell that story. The one thing I wasn't allowed to tell was the truth. I had to say I killed the man, even though it was a lie. It was my only chance, they said.

"So when we went to the hearing, that's what I had to say. I told them I couldn't remember doing it, but that I must have done it. Then they got up a whole line of witnesses. They weren't witnesses to the murder. They were character witnesses. They all said what a fine man this chicken farmer had been. And they all said I was a whore, and worse. They told all the stories about me and they made up some new ones. The prosecutor said I was a bad apple with a rotten core.

"But the fix was in. Alvin and the lawyer had worked everything out with the judge. The judge said I was a minor. He said I'd been temporarily insane when I'd done it. He said I'd be placed in a state mental hospital for observation. I found out afterward that the place I was going to was here, Mizpah."

She sat up, finished her drink, and looked hard at Owen.

"I guess there's a lot of people who still think I killed that man. Just by the fact that I'm still here. I bet you've got certain doubts yourself, huh, Owen?"

"I believe you."

"Sure you do," she said. Her bathrobe parted and he saw one white breast, a coral nipple. She laughed, covered herself, and continued her story.

"Ten years ago I moved into this room. It used to be Alvin's mother's. She was an invalid, she never went out. These are all her things, her furniture. The books are mine. Alvin brings me the books. I read whatever he brings me.

"I was so happy. Can you believe it? For the first time in my life I could relax. Alvin treated me like a princess. So did all the guards, all the patients. We had a different kind of patient then—people who could be helped. Alvin worked hard and I worked with him. I filled in as a nurse, and that's how I was treated. I ate well, I slept well, I had books and records, radio, television. And the best thing of all was that I had a wall between me and the Pines. I realized that I'd been scared for years. Scared of the men who had me whenever they wanted me. Scared of their fists and their knives and their guns. I never had to worry about that again.

"Alvin fell in love with me, and I was in love with him. He was my father, my brother, my lover, my doctor. He made me see that I was sick, and he told me how I could get better. And I did as I was told. I never broke the rules and I never complained. All I wanted to do was rest and get well. A year passed, two years, and no one said anything about leaving. I never brought up the subject."

"And here you are," said Owen.

"Here I am," she said to the canopy.

102

"Do you really think you were sick when you came here? Weren't you forced into it?"

"Owen, I was living in a wrecked car, sleeping with anybody who'd have me. I figure I had to be sick."

"But you're well now. You could leave."

"I'm not completely well."

"No?"

"No. I have my bad days. Sometimes I'm really bad, Owen."

"What's the Bad Room?"

Ruth's head jerked to one side. As she stared at Owen, a look of stark terror came into her eyes.

"Where did you hear about the Bad Room?"

"Downstairs," said Owen. "The men were talking about it. So was Alvin. You mentioned it yourself."

"Jesus, the Bad Room."

"What is it?"

Perspiration formed on Ruth's brow. "The Bad Room is where you go when you're *bad*. When you come back you're good again."

"Where is it?"

"In the basement somewhere."

"Have you been there?"

"No. Never."

"Is it solitary confinement?"

"No. I've been in isolation. It's hell. Nothing to read or write with, no one to talk to. But it's not the Bad Room. You come out of isolation and you're still yourself."

"Alvin never talked about it?"

"Not really. It's his big secret. I was never allowed in there, not even when I was a nurse. He always got a patient to help him in there, somebody who'd already been there."

103

"You're not a nurse anymore?"

"No. We don't try to cure people anymore."

"You don't?"

She shook her head, sat up, and removed the towel. While she talked she brushed her long red hair.

"Not anymore. Not since the State changed its policy with us. They used to send us local people— Pineys, people from Atlantic, Cape May counties, people who'd had breakdowns and needed rest and therapy. Then, for some reason, they changed. Now they send us the incurables, Owen. All those men downstairs have been judged criminally insane. Judges and psychiatrists say they're very sick. Most of them are."

"You mean some of them aren't?"

"Everybody here has killed somebody. Some of them have killed more than once. The sick ones don't want to get well because they'll just be sent back to jail. And the ones who aren't so sick are worried about the same thing. So everybody just gets worse. There are many levels to madness, Owen, but Mizpah gets the very bottom. We're a dumping ground. We're like those old cars people leave out there in the Pines.

"Alvin saw it coming. There was nothing he could do about it, no way of selecting people. He's had a lot of financial difficulties and he has to take the people they send him. Most of these people are so far gone that nobody cares about them, nobody comes to visit them or writes to them. Mizpah is just a prison now, a lockup. We have one real doctor, Dr. Leonard, who comes in when we call him. We get inspected once a year. The inspector doesn't look beyond the first floor. He's paid

104

off. He doesn't want to know what goes on. He doesn't care. No one cares."

"You care," said Owen.

"I used to. Now I don't. Now I'm just scared."

"Of whom, Alvin?"

"Him, myself, some of the men. See, some of the men are worried that they might be sane. If they're sane then they can be charged with murder, they think. Dorm paranoia. They think they're being watched by the authorities all the time to see if they're sane or faking. So they do things to prove they're crazy."

"What do they do?"

"They kill somebody."

"Jesus," said Owen.

"Owen, you look exhausted. Sure you don't want a drink, some coffee?"

"If you've got some coffee . . ."

Ruth made coffee in the tiny kitchenette. It was black and strong, served in a cracked cup. After drinking it, Owen's mind cleared.

"What happens when there's a murder in here?" he asked.

"There's an investigation. It lasts about half an hour. When the cops are gone the killer goes to the Bad Room and the victim is buried out back."

"Does it happen often?"

"Twice in the last five years. Once with a pair of scissors, once with an ice pick."

"And the murderers knew what they were doing?"

"Sure they did. But they didn't really get away with it, did they?"

"How do you mean?"

"They both spent a *long* time in the Bad Room. When they came out they were vegetables."

"You mean he's *operating* on them?"

"I never saw any scars. But no minds, either."

"My God!"

"I guess you saw how many idiots we have. They weren't that way when they arrived. Some of them were all right, just scared."

"He's a monster."

"He wasn't. But the Alvin I loved is gone forever."

"What changed him?"

"He had an accident," she said, shifting her eyes from Owen to the wall. "It was the men. They burnt him out, turned him into what he is now. But you should have seen him then. Jesus, we had such dreams. I was going to go to school, college, get a degree and be a nurse, maybe even a doctor. Then we were going to get married and raise a family. We'd live here and turn Mizpah into a first-class clinic. We'd do therapy and therapy research, help people, help the world. Maybe we were both just crazy, but we sure were happy with our crazy dreams. But then the State changed its policy. They turned us into a legal graveyard.

"Alvin got depressed, moody. He changed his way with me and I began to get scared. Then he had the accident and it really messed him up. Now I'm real careful with him."

"If you're frightened, why do you stay?"

"I don't know. I can't just leave Alvin. It would kill him."

"But you're a young woman, Ruth. Life's outside the walls. The world's out there."

"I don't know if I'm ready for the world. According to Rupert, nothing's changed out there. According to him, it's worse than ever."

"Rupert's your only tie with the outside?"

"Yes."

"How long has he been coming to see you?"

"Two years. He sneaked in here just like you, two years ago. I knew who he was soon as I saw him. We talked all night." Ruth laughed. "That's not all we did."

"He comes often?"

"Once or twice a month. I won't let him come more often than that. I'm scared he'll get caught. There's some bad dogs out there."

"I know."

"And the guards are worse than the dogs."

"Rupert said they're convicts."

"Well, they sure are, every one of them. Hiram Welles is a pervert, a child molester, and a sadist. Patsy Mahoney is a brute and a moron. He's doing time for armed robbery, assault, and extortion. Patsy raped me in the graveyard once. Harold Trinning is drunk all the time, and he doesn't know his own strength. We have to use them because that's who the State sends us. They're supposed to be trusties, safe men just doing their time. But they're as sick as anybody in here. They hate the men, they hate Alvin, and they hate me."

"You must be very lonely."

"There are still some of the men I can talk to. Some of them are sort of intelligent. When Rupert comes we spend the whole time talking, just like now."

"You don't talk to Alvin?"

"He talks, I listen."

"What does he talk about?"

"Himself. Alvin could talk twenty-four hours a day about himself. He's very depressed, anxious about everything. He's terribly afraid he'll lose Mizpah. He's even more afraid he'll lose me."

"Do you think he's dangerous?"

Ruth looked at Owen. "He could be."

Owen's heart beat faster. "Did he say anything to you about children? About a child?"

"I told you we planned to get married, have children."

"Yes?"

"Lately that's all he talks about. We tried for years to have a baby, but nothing happened. Then he had the accident. He's impotent now, we never make love anymore. You were right when you said I'm frustrated."

"Ruth, did he say anything to you tonight? Anything about a child?"

"Yes."

"What did he say?"

"Well, I found a puppy, a little Doberman, and I wrapped him in a blanket like a baby. We were talking and he asked me how I'd like a real baby."

"What did you say?"

"I said I'd love one. He said it was just what he wanted, too, a little boy. He said a child would make everything the way it was before. He said we could adopt one."

"Ah."

"I thought he was kidding, but he was serious. He said the State would give us a child. All we had to do was ask for one.

"That's when I knew he was dreaming again. The State of New Jersey wouldn't let a little boy within five miles of this freakhouse. Nobody in his right mind would even think of it. But Alvin was dreaming, I thought, and I let him dream. But maybe he wasn't dreaming. Maybe he's done something *bad.*"

Ruth brushed a tear from her cheek and looked away.

"Did he say anything more?"

"He said motherhood would cure me once and for all. He got very excited about it, but I had to set him straight. I spoke my mind."

"What did you tell him?"

"I said I wanted my own baby, not somebody else's. He's the one who's impotent, not me. I had Dr. Leonard check me once and I'm not sterile. I can make love all I want, have a baby, raise him myself. And I sure wouldn't want to raise one here. I told him all that and he got real quiet."

"What did he do?"

"Just stopped talking. He walked me to my door, turned around, and left without a word."

Somewhere in the big building a door slammed, a man howled, someone was running. Owen looked at Ruth. She lay on the bed staring into space. Her robe was open, her legs spread slightly. One hand rested on her white stomach, her fingers toying with red pubic hair. Silence returned. Owen stood.

"He's got my boy, Ruth," Owen whispered. "He took him to give to you, and now he knows you don't want him. The police have been here, so he knows I'm looking for my son. He's got to get rid of him, he's got to do something. I think he's out of his head. I think he's going to do something bad."

"He could be waiting for you, Owen. He may already know you're here."

"I don't care."

"Owen, he could do something to you. He could change you so you wouldn't know where you are, why you came here, or even *who* you are."

"Nobody could do that. Not to me."

"I've seen it. I've seen big strong men turned into dogs."

Owen was trembling. He looked deeply into Ruth's eyes. "Do you think he would do anything to Robin?"

She looked away.

"Answer me!"

"Well, he might. See, he *believes* in the Bad Room. He thinks he's doing people a favor. . . ."

"Christ, I've got to get down there," Owen spat out, turning to the door.

"Wait!" Ruth sat up in bed, closed her robe. "Owen, I'll go with you."

"You'll help me?" Owen asked.

"Yes. If you'll help me."

"I'll get you out of here."

"Let's go."

As Ruth stood, someone knocked on the door, three hard loud knocks.

"Who is it?" Ruth looked frightened.

"Open up, Ruth," said a harsh voice.

"I'm in bed, Alvin. Give me a minute."

There was a pause, the sound of men talking. Then came a rustle and the clicking of a key in the lock.

Chapter Six

RUTH RAN to the door and bolted it.

"He's got the guards with him," she whispered. "Hide!"

"Where?"

"In there. Quick!" She pointed to the door at the far end of the room. Owen ran to it and stepped through. He was in a small hallway with an open door on either side. On the right was a bathroom with toilet and washbasin. On the left was a dark empty room. Owen stepped into it and pulled the door shut with a click.

The room, like those Owen had seen below, was entirely padded—floor, ceiling, walls, and door. Set in the door was a small window which opened and closed. In the wall opposite was a barred window through which moonlight filtered faintly.

With his ear to the small opening, Owen could hear Ruth release the bolt. Footsteps sounded heavily, men moving quickly into and about the room.

"Alvin, I'm not dressed. . . ."

"Are you all right, Ruth?" It was Alvin's voice, deep, loud, resonant.

"I'm fine. What's the matter?"

"We've got an intruder. Someone's prowling around."

"Well, nobody's here, nobody's been here, and nobody's coming here. I'm exhausted and I'm going to bed. So get your guards out of here, Alvin."

"They've got to search, Ruth. I'm sorry. Welles, check back there."

Owen settled in a dark corner when he heard the hallway door open. Outside, a guard snapped the bathroom light on and off. An arm reached through the square hole in the door, a flashlight clicked on. The beam came near Owen and he tucked in his toes. The light went off.

"Nobody back here, Doctor," said the guard.

"Nobody here," said another.

"Check the second floor again, Mahoney. Welles, you take the first. If you find anything, give a shout."

"Want me to call the Troopers, doc?"

"No. We'll handle this ourselves. Get going, both of you. Trinning, you wait outside."

The steel door slammed shut and for a moment there was quiet. Then, "Someone's been here, Ruth."

"No one's been here."

"You're lying."

"Alvin, you listen to me—"

"No! You listen to me! I'm still in charge here and I must be obeyed. I won't have things going on behind my back."

"You're shouting at me, Alvin."

"You won't listen, Ruth! You don't hear a word I say anymore. Will you listen?"

"If you lower your voice."

"The police were here tonight. Chief Howzer of the State Troopers. They're looking for a man, a prowler. He said the man might be headed here."

"Why? Why would anybody want to poke around here?"

"I don't know. But someone has gotten inside. We found his shoes on the first floor."

"Calm down, Alvin."

"Someone's been in this room, Ruth. I can smell him."

"You're wrong, Alvin. You're torturing yourself. I don't let anyone in here but you."

"That's a lie! You had someone up here last week. And it wasn't the first time, was it? You've been entertaining someone up here for some time. Admit it."

"Who? Who would I entertain?"

"How am I supposed to know? One of the guards, one of the men?"

"Alvin, you're being silly."

"Am I? Remember Roberts, the guard?"

"That was four years ago, Alvin. Maybe *five.*"

"That was the one I happened to catch you with. I know there have been others. You're really insatiable, you know. Just like always. You're as sick as you were the day you came in here! Look what I've done for you. I've done everything for you that can possibly be done. I've offered you marriage, a home, a career . . ."

"I don't want a career."

"So you said. You want to have a child. I told you I could arrange that."

"I don't want you to 'arrange' anything!"

"What *do* you want?"

"I want to get the hell out of here."

There was a long pause, then Alvin spoke. His voice lacked the force and resonance it held before.

"You want to leave?"

"Yes."

"Why?"

"I want to live, Alvin. I want to stop dreaming."

"You're not ready."

"Yes I am."

"You wouldn't last a day outside."

"Yes I would."

"Where would you go?"

"Far away."

"Where?"

"California."

"Who have you been talking to, Ruth?"

"No one."

"Who have you been sleeping with, Ruthie? Who's been giving it to you?"

"No one."

"I can't remember the last time we made love."

"That's not my fault, Alvin."

"I know you can't get along without it. I remember."

"That's all behind me. I've grown up."

"No you haven't. You're a child. You always will be. You're a nymphomaniac, Ruth."

"You told me there was no such thing, remember?"

"You proved me wrong, Ruth. Your case should go in the books."

"You're being very nasty, Alvin. Do you know that?"

"I love you."

"You don't sound like it."

"I love you. Do you still love me?"

"Of course I do."

"Take off that bathrobe."

"What will that do?"

"Just take it off. I want to see you."

114

"I don't want to. Not when you're like this."

"Are you going to obey me?"

"Stop shouting!"

"ARE YOU GOING TO OBEY?"

"Go to hell."

Owen heard a loud slap, Ruth's cry. It was followed by a thud and more slaps. He heard the steel door open, Alvin's voice.

"Trinning! Get in here and help me! Miss Sooey is having a fit."

There were footsteps, running. Ruth screamed in protest, furniture overturned.

"Strip her! Get her downstairs."

Cloth tearing, Ruth shouting obscenities.

Owen decided to act. He tried the door. It was locked. He put his shoulder to it and pushed. The door did not budge. He ran at it with both arms straight out before him. The door held. It was steel, strong and solid, and it would open only with a key.

Owen heard Ruth scuffling with the guard. A door slammed. All was quiet.

It was hot in the padded cell. The barred window would not open. The canvas, which covered every surface, was warm and clammy to the touch. The darkness was nearly total.

Owen felt his pocket for the keys, then remembered he'd left them outside in Ruth's room. He reached through the small, rectangular opening in the door, his hand feeling in all directions. The lock was a few inches beyond his reach.

He was a prisoner.

The only person who knew he was there was Ruth Sooey. Owen decided he would sit tight, remain calm, and wait till Ruth came back or Rupert showed up with the police. There was nothing to do but wait.

Waiting was the one thing Owen did not want to do. Robin was in Mizpah, probably locked away in the dark basement, frightened out of his wits. Alvin, his captor, was running around the asylum half out of his mind. And he, Owen, could do nothing about it but sit and stare at padded walls.

Owen closed his eyes and prayed.

God, he prayed, I've done everything I can. Help me.

Sleep came, but it was short, shallow, night-mared.

When he opened his eyes the room was lighter. A gray dawn light came through the little window. He went to it and looked out. He was facing the grounds to the rear of the building. Quite clearly he could see the little cemetery beneath the willow, the black rectangle of the open grave. A morning mist obscured the tops of the pines, flowed over the white walls, and drifted in patches over the weedy field.

How long had he slept?

He walked to the window in the door.

"Ruth? Ruth Sooey?"

There was no answer.

Where was she? Where were Rupert and the Troopers? Where was Robin?

"ROBIN!"

His own voice frightened him. It was hoarse, cracked, full of fear and panic. And no one but he could hear it.

He returned to the barred window, looking out. Nothing had changed. He reached through the bars and with his fist tried to break the glass. It was very thick and would not break.

Then he saw it. High above the pines, above the cloud-sea of morning mist, was the watchtower. The glass walls of the observation room looked black, vacant, lifeless. Yet behind them men were watching. The rangers, Bob and Bill, were up there with the overview. Like the old gods they stood there, looking down.

Laughing. Impotent.

Owen stared at the black windows and they looked back at him like eyes looking into his soul. He trembled.

Below him, near the base of the building, a man stepped into view. He was old, stooped, and bald. He wore torn sneakers and a threadbare, ill-fitting blue suit. Around his neck was a wrinkled black tie. In his hand he carried a small bouquet of wild flowers and weeds. He stooped to add more weeds to the bouquet.

Owen tried to pound on the little window, but the bars prevented him from making any noise.

The old man, obviously an inmate, was joined by two others. Each wore a soiled suit, a black tie. The bald one showed the others where to gather flowers. Soon the three of them held bouquets. They stood quietly, looking down, not talking to one another. They faced the base of the building, just out of Owen's sight.

Owen saw a guard, a large man with a protruding stomach, standing nearby. Leashed to his left hand were the two Doberman pinschers, sitting licking their paws. His right hand rested on a long black billy club. He looked bored.

More men, young and old, joined the scene. Owen recognized some of them from the night before. They wore their battered shoes, their soiled, unpressed suits, their black ties. They were serious, quiet, and grave. They carried their small bouquets and stared at the ground.

Owen heard a door open.

He ran to the hole in the door.

"Hello!" he shouted. "Who's there?"

He heard the door open all the way, then close. He heard footsteps, slow and stumbling, in Ruth's apartment.

"Hello!" he shouted. "Back here!"

The door to the hallway opened.

"Huh?" said a man's voice.

"I'm in here," said Owen. "I'm locked in. Let me out."

A man's face appeared. It was old, lined, and grinning toothlessly.

"Who're you?" the man asked Owen.

"I'm a doctor," said Owen. "Let me out."

The old man stopped smiling, shook his head.

"You ain't no doctor," he said, spitting on the floor.

Owen saw that he wore pajamas, just like his.

"Come on," said Owen, "let me out."

"How am I supposed to do that?" The old man looked genuinely worried.

"Look. Look at the lock," said Owen. He reached through the little window as far as he could and pointed. "There. What do you see?"

"A key," said the old man. "I see a key." The old man reached out, made a noise, held up a heavy brass key.

Owen made a grab for it. The old man jerked it away.

"Give me the key," Owen said.

"Uh-uh. You're no doctor and you get no key."

"What's your name?" Owen smiled.

"Welter."

"Welter, give me the key and I'll get you out of here. I swear I'll get you out of here."

"Out of where?"

"Mizpah."

"I don't want to get out of Mizpah. Do you?"

"Yes. I don't belong here. I'm—"

"That's your problem, fella," said the old man. He winked, turned, and stepped out of Owen's sight. Owen could hear him puttering around in Ruth's room.

"Come back!"

"I'm busy," Welter said.

"What are you doing?"

"Emptying Miss Sooey's tub."

"What did you do with the key?"

"Got it right here in my pocket."

"Welter, for the love of God will you give me the key?"

"Nope. That key goes to Dr. Alvin."

"God damn it, Welter!"

"Hey, you better watch it in there. We don't stand for swearing in here. Vilification."

The old man reappeared, carrying a bucket of water. He opened the door opposite Owen's and poured the water in the toilet. He turned to face Owen.

"Get your arm out of that hole."

Owen withdrew his arm. Welter came close to the door, made a sound in the lock.

"We don't use the name of the Lord in vain in here," he said, moving out of view.

Owen looked through the hole. On the wall of the bathroom was a mirror. Owen could see himself in the mirror, a frantic face in a square hole. Below the hole was the lock and in the lock was

119

the key. Owen reached through the hole, strained, but could not touch it.

"Welter?"

"What?" Welter appeared with another bucket of water. He saw Owen's hand inches from the key. He laughed and poured the water in the toilet.

"Welter, I'm sorry."

"That's a commandment."

"I know," said Owen. "I'm sorry. I'm new here."

"Okay."

"Welter? Welter, what's going on outside?"

"Where?" Welter was in the other room.

"Out back. There are men out there in suits. Is that the funeral?"

"You got it."

"I want to go to the funeral."

"Too bad."

"Welter, why aren't you going to the funeral?"

"I never go."

"Never?"

"I went once. Never again."

Owen walked over to the barred window, looked out. The men had moved to the little cemetery. They stood facing each other across the open grave, waiting patiently.

"Welter? How come you have funerals here?"

"How do you mean?" Welter's tone was friendlier. He dumped a bucket of water in the toilet, looked at Owen through the hole.

"I don't understand, Welter. Miss Sooey says the funeral is just a game."

"Some game," said Welter, not moving.

"Tell me about it."

"The funerals? The Mizpah funerals?"

120

"Yes. Tell me about the Mizpah funerals. How did they get started?"

"They started when somebody died."

"Who, Welter. Who died?"

"One of the vegetables. He got killed."

"How?"

"Was before I came here. But he got knifed, I think."

"What happened?"

"Well, Dr. Alvin, he decided to bury the man out back with his parents."

"Whose parents?"

"Dr. Alvin's. His mother and father are buried out there."

"Go on."

"Well, when he buried him he had a funeral, like the one going on now. The men liked the service, I guess. There's been a funeral every month since."

"Every month?"

"Every month, full moon."

"It's just a pretend funeral."

"You got it, fella. It's a fake funeral. Some of the guys live for it."

"Do they ever have a real body?"

"Sometimes."

"They do? When?"

"When somebody dies. We had another killing in here a year back. And a guard died. They both got funerals. They're both out there."

Welter moved away. Owen could hear him in Ruth's room, washing dishes in the kitchenette. He walked back to the barred window. What he saw next made his blood run cold.

Four inmates, acting as pallbearers, emerged from the building carrying a coffin. It was crude, homemade, painted white. It was a very small coffin.

A child's coffin.

Owen's eyes bulged. He blinked and looked again. The pallbearers moved slowly along the winding path to the cemetery. They walked slowly, sadly, their feet dragging. The coffin shifted from side to side as the men carried it closer to the dark hole.

"Welter!" Owen ran to the door. "Welter!"

"Yeah." Welter washed the dishes, sounded bored.

"Welter! Look out the window!"

"I'm looking, Bub."

"Welter, do you see what they're carrying, can you see the coffin?"

"I see it."

"It's a *child's* coffin."

"Looks it."

"Welter, come here."

"Uh-uh."

"Come here, please, Welter."

"I'm on the job."

"Welter, have you heard anything about a child? A child in here? A little boy?"

"Hell, no."

"Welter, what are you doing?"

"Sweeping up."

"Welter, come here where I can see you."

"I'll get there."

Owen ran back to the window. At the head of the grave was the little monkey-faced man from the dormitory, Patruzi. He stood with an open Bible in his hands, reading from it. He pointed to the coffin, to the sky, to the deep hole. He pointed to

122

the inmates, who bowed their heads, wept, wrung their hands.

Several yards apart from the group stood the stone-faced guard, holding the dogs. He looked once at the raving inmates, scratched his stomach, and yawned.

"Welter?"

"How you doing?" Welter's smiling face was at the hole in the door. Owen moved toward him, talking.

"Welter, nobody knows I'm here. I got locked in here by mistake. I was kidding about being a doctor. I'm a patient, just like you."

"I figured," said the old man.

"I'm new, but I've already met some of the boys. I know Patruzi, out there. I know Cebulski, I know all the guards . . ." Owen was a yard away, inching in.

"You know the director?"

"Yes!" said Owen, an arm's length away. "I know Dr. Alvin. He's my friend."

"Serves you right. Ha!" Welter smiled sweetly, his weathered face framed in the square hole.

"I'm in here by mistake, Welter. Unlock the door and we'll both go see the director."

"You're in there by mistake?"

"Sure! I was just walking around and got locked in. I'm new. I don't know my way around."

"What did you do?"

"How do you mean, Welter?"

"What did you do to get yourself put away in here? Who did you kill?"

"My father, Welter. I killed my father."

"That'll do it," said Welter.

"Welter, open the door and we'll go see the director."

123

"I'll go get him." Welter turned away.

"Wait! Welter, don't go away." Owen stepped closer, his hand below the opening.

Welter's face returned, still smiling.

Owen acted. His hand shot out, reaching for the old man's throat. Welter jerked his head back. Owen reached blindly through the opening, catching Welter's sleeve. Owen could hear the flimsy material tearing away. He could hear Welter swearing.

"You son of a bitch!" yelled the old man, swinging his broom against the opening. Owen grabbed for the broom. His fingers closed on straw. Pulling hard, he jerked the broom from Welter's hand.

"Give that back here!" Welter said, keeping far back from the door.

Owen looked through the hole. In the bathroom mirror he could see his arm, the broom, the keyhole, and the key. Taking the broom by the handle he lowered it until it touched the key.

"Don't you try that," said Welter, coming closer.

"Get back, Welter," said Owen, "or I'll kill you."

Welter crouched, came closer.

Watching the mirror, Owen pushed the broom down hard over the key, then levered it outward from the lock. The key fell to the floor. Owen guided the broom down and behind it, ready to sweep it under the door.

But Welter's hand darted out, grabbed the key. He stood, smiled, shook his head.

"Drop the broom," he said to Owen.

Owen let it fall.

Welter threw the key in the toilet and flushed

it. He looked down into the bowl, then back at Owen.

"Won't flush," he said.

"Welter . . ."

"When they want to let you out," said the old man with a shrug, "you tell them where the key's at, huh?"

"Welter . . ."

"You shut up." The door to the hallway closed.

"WELTER!"

Owen's knees would not stop shaking. He clung to the bars and watched through the window.

The pallbearers slung ropes beneath the little white coffin and suspended it over the hole. As it hung there the inmates shrieked and tore at their hair.

"Welter?" Owen's voice was racked with sobs. "They're burying a child out there."

"Aw, shut up," was the muffled reply.

As the coffin was slowly lowered, the inmates tore at their weed bouquets and tossed them onto the lid. As the coffin dipped below the level of the ground, it moved.

The coffin jerked.

Owen gagged, bent low, came up coughing.

"Welter! He's alive!"

"I saw it."

"What? What did you see, Welter?"

"I saw the coffin move."

"He's alive, they're burying him alive!"

"Wouldn't be the first time."

"What?"

The old man was back in the hallway, looking through the opening. When Owen turned he stepped back. Owen turned back to the window, his hand at the bars.

"I said it wouldn't be the first time," Welter said.

"First time for what?"

"First time they buried somebody . . . alive."

"Who?"

"Let's see. It was last year. It was full moon, time for a funeral. Some of the boys got pretty heated up and there was a fight. It was a big fight, almost everybody was in it. A guard got hurt breaking it up. One guy was sent to the Bad Room. And Dr. Alvin said he was going to punish the rest of us. He said we couldn't have the funeral."

Owen's eyes were riveted on the open grave. Patruzi, handing the Bible to another inmate, picked up a shovel and slowly poured soil into the hole, his mouth working. Welter's voice continued in the background, but Owen was only half-conscious of the old man's words.

"Now, as for me, I don't give a shit for funerals. I'm going to be cremated when the time comes, and that's all. But the boys here take these things seriously. It's all some of them talk about. And when they found out about the funeral being called off they got pretty mad. They got *bad* mad."

"They're burying my boy alive," said Owen.

"Yeah. Well, what the boys did that day was rough. They grabbed somebody during recreation—I don't say who—and they dragged him over to the cemetery. Grave was already dug, all ready. There was some of them keeping the guards occupied, and some of them nailing down the lid on the guy."

"They're filling in the hole!" said Owen.

"Right. Well, they buried the guy six feet deep and filled it in. The coffin was jumping and jerking, just like that one, only more 'cause it was full size. He must have got the gag loose because you could hear him yelling for a while. You could hear him four, five feet under. When it was full up you could put your ear to the ground and still hear him."

Owen's legs buckled. He sank to the floor and sat staring at Welter's face in the little rectangle.

"Was Miss Sooey who saved him. She heard about it from one of the men and she went and got the guards. They got him out pretty quick. He was passed out cold, blood all over him."

"Welter?"

"I'd say he was down there an hour before they got to him. That's a pretty long time to be buried when you're not dead, huh?"

"Welter, listen to me—"

"You ask me, the guards knew all along. They don't give a shit. It was Miss Sooey made them dig."

Owen, on his hands and knees, crawled toward Welter. Saliva dripped from Owen's mouth as he tried to speak.

". . . please?"

Welter moved away.

"Oh, please, God?"

Welter's voice came from the other room. "Hey look, Bub! Look at them now, those fools. They're dancing on that grave!"

Waves of nausea washed over Owen as he lay prostrate on the soiled canvas floor, coughing and retching, sobbing and babbling deliriously. Wracked by stomach spasms, convulsions, and a bone-crushing headache, he lost all track of time, place, and, finally, identity. At the end there was no Owen, no Mizpah, no child buried alive by madmen. There was no light or color, no sound, no movement, nothing but pain, terror, and anxiety. Owen was conscious of nothing.

But he was not unconscious. Something in him refused to give in to shock, to the soothing veils of darkness that closed over him, then opened suddenly. A part of him lay in reserve, ready to regain control, to think and to act. The rest of him tried to die.

Jumping to his feet, Owen flung himself at the door, then the walls, the barred window, the floor itself. Owen tore his fingernails on the heavy canvas, but got nowhere. His sanity fleeing him, Owen curled himself into a ball and screamed gibberish, animal sounds.

"Owen?"

Owen stopped screaming at the sound of his name.

"Owen?"

Everything was a blur. Owen tried to focus, to direct, to address himself to the sound. Lying on his back, he saw a blurred face in the little window.

"Welter?"

"Owen, it's me. Rupert."

Rupert?

Owen rolled over, pushed himself up on his hands and knees, crawled to the door.

"Rupert?"

"You okay, Owen?"

"Rupert, is that you?"

"It's me, Owen. Hey, are you okay?"

"Let me out."

"How do I do that?"

Owen pounded his temples with his fists,

rubbed his eyes. Slowly his brain began to function.

"Key's in the toilet. Quick."

Rupert fished the key from the toilet bowl and turned it in the lock. Owen staggered out, his face distorted with rage, frustration, and despair. He pushed past Rupert, slipped, and fell. He crawled through Ruth's apartment, his eyes on the open door. Rupert ran to him, helped him to his feet.

"You'll never make it down those stairs alone, Owen. Let me help."

Owen leaned on Rupert and together they descended the iron stairs.

"Where we going, Owen?"

"Out back."

"What if somebody sees us?"

"I don't care."

When they got to the heavy ground-level door, Rupert peeked out.

"Nobody's around, Owen."

Owen pushed past him, shielding his eyes from the sunlight. With his strength and reason returning, Owen directed his footsteps down the sandy path to the cemetery. Halfway there he began to trot. Then he was running, jumping over clumps of weeds, his bare feet flashing. Rupert was not far behind.

The soil on the fresh grave was covered with footprints. Stuck in the center was a coat hanger that someone had bent in the shape of a cross. Propped against the wall were the two shovels. Owen handed one to Rupert and with the other began to dig.

"What are we after, Owen?"

"My boy."

"Jesus, Owen, he's down there?"

"Dig."

They dug, the soft earth flying over their shoulders. Rupert stopped to look around. They were alone.

"What did they do to him, Owen?"

"They buried him. They buried him alive."

"Alive? He's alive down there?"

"Dig!"

Sandy soil filled the air as the two men worked in silent frenzy. The little coffin was buried deep and many minutes passed before they were down to it. Owen's shovel struck the coffin and he shouted, "Robin!"

"Shh . . ." said Rupert. "Somebody's looking out a window."

"Help me."

They dug with their hands, working under the box, prying it from the earth. When it was free Owen used the shovel to pry open the lid. It was crudely fashioned and the paint was still wet. It tore away. Over Owen's shoulder Rupert looked down into the box.

"That's no little boy," he said.

Owen's eyes blurred, refocused.

It was not Robin.

It was the dog, the little Doberman puppy. And it was alive, breathing faintly.

Owen howled.

Chapter Seven

WHEN RUPERT touched the puppy it twitched. Its eyes opened slightly. Owen picked it up and held it to his chest. The dog widened one eye and looked at Owen. It licked Owen's fingers. It licked the tears from his cheeks. Owen sat with the dog, trembling, rocking to and fro, weeping uncontrollably.

"Where's Robie?" he pleaded.

"Shhhh!" said Rupert. On tiptoes, Rupert was peeking over the rim of the grave.

"What," said Owen.

"Guards."

"Close by?"

"Over by the house. They got the dogs." Rupert ducked low. He looked closely at Owen, put his hands on Owen's shoulders, and said, "Do you still think he's here?"

"Yes."

"Then we've got to get to him."

"Yes."

"Pull yourself together, Owen."

"I'm trying."

"Don't quit." Rupert took another look over the edge and withdrew his head quickly.

"They coming toward us?" Owen asked.

"They're looking this way. They're going to see the grave's been dug up."

"How far away?"

"Fifty feet."

At that moment the puppy sneezed. Owen tried to cover its snout with his hand. The dog jumped from his arms and tried to scramble up the loose earth. It was weak and having difficulty moving its legs, but it was getting away. Owen grabbed it. The dog yelped in surprise, turned, and bit Owen's hand. Released, the puppy sprang to the rim of the hole and stood there making the strange low sound that only a Doberman pup can make. Its teeth were bared, its black eyes wild, focused on Owen.

"Goddamn dog," said Owen.

"Guards are coming, Owen. Coming fast."

"Let's go." Owen began to climb from the hole.

"Where?"

"Over the gate!"

The guards stopped at the sight of Owen and Rupert climbing from the grave.

"What the hell?"

"Go!" shouted Owen, pointing to the left. He ran to the right, his legs pumping. Over his shoulder he saw Rupert heading for the side of the madhouse, a huge heavyset guard lumbering after him. Behind Owen ran Patsy, the guard from the dormitory. Leashed, the two Dobermans ran with him. Then Patsy stopped and released the dogs.

"Git 'im!" screamed the guard.

Owen made it to the rusty gates with the dogs at his heels. He leaped to the bars and climbed frantically, the dogs jumping high into the air, snapping at his flesh.

Owen struggled over the rusted, curving, pointed tops of the bars. They caught at his pajamas, but he tore himself free. At the top, with one step and a jump between him and freedom, he stopped.

On the lawn stood two guards. Between them, cowering under a torrent of kicks and blows, was Rupert. Over him was a thick ring-net, a throwing net for mad dogs. Rupert shrieked, begging for the beating to stop.

Owen looked at the road that would take him back to Zion Road, to the camper, to a telephone. He looked below him at the furiously snarling dogs, waiting to rip into him, tear him apart like a rabbit.

"Daddy!"

Owen's head snapped up. A child's voice had come from somewhere in the insane asylum.

"ROBIN!"

There was no answer.

A pistol shot cracked the morning air, a bullet flew by Owen's head. Owen jumped.

He landed on the larger of the two dogs, the male. He slammed his fist into the dog's head, stunning it. The female sprang for his throat. Owen jumped out of the way and the dog's teeth clicked on air. Owen kicked it as it flew by, catching it in the stomach, lifting it from the ground. The male, still dazed from Owen's blow, tried to attack. Owen dodged and sprang to the gate. He was nearly to the top when the enraged dog leaped. Owen swung out blindly, his fist catching the side of the dog's head, deflecting it onto the rusted spikes. Hanging from its torn and bloody jaws, unable to breathe, the Doberman yelped once and died. The female howled, turned from Owen, and tried to climb the bars to its mate.

133

Owen heard another shot, then Alvin's voice, ordering them to stop shooting.

Owen ran for the guards.

They faced him, brandishing their clubs. Rupert, on the ground between them, was still. The guards looked at Owen, charging through the shallow pond, and smiled.

"Come on, goon," said one of them, slapping his truncheon on his palm. "Come and get it."

"Come on, you crazy motherfucker," said the other.

"Leave him be," shouted Alvin from the porch. "Don't hurt him!"

The guards backed away. Owen ran to Rupert's inert body, lifted the big ring-net, and knelt by his side. Rupert was unconscious, congealed blood matting his hair and drying on his face. But he was alive and breathing. Owen looked up at Alvin, thirty feet away.

"Where's my son?" he asked, walking toward the porch.

Alvin did not reply. He stood expressionless while Owen, bloody, ragged, crazed from the fight, crossed the lawn. Owen's arms were spread before him, his fingers splayed. Behind Alvin, peeking from windows on both floors, were the distorted faces of the inmates, their hands at the bars.

"Where's Robin?" he demanded, mounting the concrete steps. He was a few yards from the director when a guard threw the net.

A billy club crashed onto his head and Owen went down. The last thing he saw was Alvin squatting beside him, preparing a hypodermic needle.

"You killed a dog," he said, shaking his head. He put the needle into Owen's arm. "That was bad," he said, looking at the guards, then back at Owen. *"Bad."*

Owen awoke to total darkness. He was lying on his stomach on a concrete floor, unable to move his arms. He squirmed, rolled over on his back. Something hard and sharp dug into the small of his back. He rolled to his side. His arms were pinned behind him. He lay on his stomach, letting his head clear.

"Owen?" It was Rupert's voice.

"Rupert."

"You okay, Owen?"

"Rupert, did you hear him?"

"Who?"

"Robin. He called to me, I heard him call when they were beating you."

"I didn't hear him."

"He's here. Oh, Jesus God, he's here . . ."

"Owen, are you okay?"

"I can't move my arms."

"Me neither. They got us in straitjackets."

"Oh my God."

"You've been out for hours. I thought you were dead."

"Where are we?"

"I don't know. In the basement I guess."

"Are you okay?"

"I think I got a busted rib. Hurts every time I take a breath. They got this straitjacket on me so tight."

"Maybe I could get it off you," said Owen. "I could use my teeth."

"No good. It's got a padlock on the back. They got us, Owen."

"Don't give up."

"They could do anything with us now. I don't like not being able to move my arms."

"Don't think about it."

"I'm claustrophobic, Owen."

"Put it out of your mind."

"How can I?"

"Think about something else."

"What?"

"The Troopers. How come you didn't bring the police like I told you?"

"Owen, I never had the chance, honest."

"Why not?"

"What happened was I got the dogs so riled up at the gates that a guard came to have a look. He was going to unlock the gates, let the dogs out, so I had to run. I ran all the way around the back to the willow and I climbed up it to have a look. I saw the lights on all over the place and a lot of screaming and yelling. It sounded like something terrible was happening. I got so scared, Owen. Then I saw a light on in Ruthie's room, and the candle is a signal that she wants to see me. I didn't tell you I've been seeing her."

"I know all about it. I met her, talked to her."

"It's a secret I've kept for two years. I've never told a soul."

"Go on."

"Well, when things quieted down I went over the wall. I figured if I could get to Ruthie I could find out what was going on. I figured if you were caught I could get to a phone in there, call the police."

"The phones are switched off."

"Oh. . . . I got to the stairway for Ruthie's room, but it was locked. I was real worried about the dogs, so I got to another door as quick as I

136

could, and it was open. I tried every door in that stairway, but they were all locked. Guards were running in and out, so I hid under the stairs. And what happened was I fell asleep. I didn't want to, but it happened. When I woke up it was dawn and everything was unlocked. I got up to Ruthie's room and found you. How did you get locked up?"

In a few words Owen told Rupert everything that had happened. At the end of his story something made him pause. "Rupert, somebody's been screwing around with my mind. I was supposed to think they were burying my boy alive. Who would do something like that to a human being?"

"I don't know."

"It was Ruth who told me to hide in that room."

"Owen, you met her, you talked to her; you don't think she'd do that, do you?"

"No."

"Then who?"

"Alvin. He was getting rough with her. He must have gotten her to tell him where I was. He knows this place, every inch of it. He knew I had a good view of that cemetery back there. He let me sit there."

"Why?"

"He knows I'm after my boy. He got someone to make that little coffin, just Robin's size. He got them to put the dog in it and he let them go. And then he sent Welter up there to torture me."

"But why, Owen?"

"I guess he figured I'd snap."

"Go crazy?"

"I almost did. I almost broke down completely. Nobody will ever know what I went through up there. It was torture. If I cracked he could just

137

shut me away forever. Like your sister. And then he could do what he liked with Robin."

"He's crazy."

"You should have heard him with your sister."

"We've got to help her. We've got to get her and Robin and—"

At that moment a key rattled noisily in the lock and the door flew open. In rushed a black-and-tan snarling Doberman, straining at a heavy chain leash. Holding the dog back with both arms and the weight of his thick body was Patsy.

"That's him, Eva," said the guard, pointing at Owen. *"That's the son of a bitch killed Adolf!"*

The dog went for Owen, but the guard held it back. Owen rolled to the wall, hiding his face. Patsy let the dog to within a few inches of Owen's neck, and laughed as the dog barked frantically, half-choked by the chain.

"Goon meat, huh? You want some goon meat, girl?"

"Don't!" screamed Owen, feeling the dog's breath on his neck.

"Shut up, goon!"

"Leave him alone!" shouted Rupert.

Patsy jerked the dog away from Owen, dragged it over to Rupert, and kicked him in the side. Rupert cried out in agony. The dog sank its teeth into the heavy canvas of the straitjacket, but the guard pulled it off.

"He's hurt," pleaded Owen. "He has a broken rib."

"Tell that to the dog, goon!"

Owen tried to stand. He got as far as his knees before dizziness overcame him and he fell forward, unable to break the fall with his hands. His face smacked the concrete floor. Patsy laughed.

138

"We're gonna have some real fun with you nuts," yelled the guard. "You wait."

"Patsy," Owen gasped, "the police are looking for me. I've got money, I can pay you—"

Patsy kicked Owen hard in the stomach. The straitjacket was so tightly bound that Owen nearly suffocated regaining his breath. While he struggled, Patsy shouted at him.

"You killed Adolf, you pervert! And now Eva's gone crazy. She's stone crazy, goon, and you did it to her!"

"Please . . ." said Owen.

Owen saw the slobbering jaws snap inches away from his face. The dog's bark was loud, but Owen could hear Patsy goading it on. He rolled to the wall, praying the guard would not let the dog on him.

"Wanna see what this bitch can do, goon? You wanna see?"

"No!" begged Owen, shaking his head.

"Anybody'd kill a dog gets no sympathy from me, huh? Not now, not ever, you hear? Dogs are the only good thing in here."

Owen lay silent and still, trying to pray, but no words reached him through his pain, confusion, and terror.

"Director says I got to shoot this dog, huh? Dog's no good no more. I raised her from a pup, her and Adolf, and now I got to shoot her, huh?"

"Don't . . ."

Patsy let the dog on Owen. The Doberman, given a few extra inches of chain, ripped its fangs into Owen's thigh. Owen screamed and the guard pulled the dog off him.

"Dog's a killer now, huh? She'd take you apart under a minute! Maybe I'll leave her with you

139

awhile. So's you can make friends, huh? Want to make friends with Eva, goon? Want me to leave her with you while I go get the shotgun? Huh?"

Owen shook his head.

Patsy heaved at the chain and dragged the hysterical dog across the floor and through the door.

"I'll leave her outside, huh? So's you can hear her go mad! And I don't want to hear no talking in here, huh? I hear talking and I let her in."

Patsy's voice was choked with emotion. He slammed the door, locking it. The dog continued to bark and claw the metal door.

Rupert rolled across the floor until he touched Owen. He whispered in Owen's ear, "How are you doing?"

"I don't know. I think I'm bleeding."

Rupert put his cheek against Owen's thigh.

"It's bloody, but it's not gushing out or anything. You're not going to bleed to death. Listen to that dog."

"That dog is crazy."

"Maybe we shouldn't talk."

"Nobody can hear us over that dog."

"You think he'd let her in on us, Owen?"

"No. He would have done it. He has orders not to hurt us."

"He hurt us."

"We're okay."

"God, I can't stand having my arms pinned this way. It's driving me nuts."

"Hang on."

"For what, Owen? Who's going to help us?"

"Maybe the Troopers. Maybe they'll come back."

"Not likely. Mizpah's a state institution. So are

the Troopers. They've got the same boss: Trenton. The Troopers don't mess with Mizpah."

"Howzer was here."

"He knows Alvin. They're old friends. When they had the big scandal here, Howzer covered it up. He was in on the fix; still is. If he knew we were down here he'd laugh."

"What scandal?"

"Didn't Ruthie tell you?"

"No."

"It happened before she got here, when I was a little kid."

"You'd better lower your voice."

"It happened when I was a little kid. Mizpah was private then, a private rest home for old folks, whatever, anybody who could pay. Anyway, a man escaped, ran away. He made it back to his family up in Burlington County. He said bad things were going on here, real bad things. They were starving people, beating them, everything, and they had all the patients too terrified to talk, see?

"The place was owned by Alvin's father then, but it was run by the guards. The old man never knew what was going on. So when the scandal hit and the investigators came out here, Alvin's father almost went to jail. Almost. But the story is that he gave everything he had to Howzer, and Howzer used it to pay off somebody big in Trenton. It all blew over. The old man died a few months later and Alvin sold the place out to the state."

"Christ Almighty."

"So I don't think Chief Howzer's any big hope."

"You don't think he'd come if we called him?"

"I wouldn't bet on it. He's a crook. This isn't the

141

only place that kicks back to him. And the people who get in his way are in big trouble."

"Better not talk so loud."

"Big trouble, Owen. Chief Howzer killed a man."

"He did?"

"Killed him in the jail. Covered it all up."

Something slammed into the door. It was Eva. After a short pause there came another loud slam, then weak growling and barking.

"It's trying to break down the door, Owen."

"Forget about the dog."

"I never saw such a bloodthirsty animal."

"Rupert, how about the rangers?"

"Bob and Bill? What would they care?"

"They know about me, about Robin. They know I'm running around somewhere, and they know all about this place."

"Forget it."

"We could start a fire, Rupert. Those weeds would burn like paper."

"Owen, I swear if a fire broke out inside the walls they'd let us burn to the ground. You, me, Ruthie, your little boy; they'd let us burn."

"Why do you say that?"

"They're nuts."

"That's your answer for everything. They didn't seem crazy to me."

"No?"

"Well, they seemed a little funny."

"They're batty, Owen. They've been up that tower too long."

"What do you mean?"

"All I know is what I've seen with my own eyes. When I was about ten years old, I was playing out behind the bar, in the backyard, and Bill came by on his way from their cabin. He was heading for the tower and he asked me if I'd ever been up there. I said no. He said he'd show me how it works. So up I went with him. My mom and dad are both dead drunk inside the bar, and I'm up the fire tower with Bob and Bill."

Suddenly, Owen began to breathe heavily, gasping for each breath. He fought to regain control and won.

"Owen! You okay?"

"Just catching my breath. They got this thing on so tight I can hardly breathe. What about Bob and Bill?"

"They got me up there with their instruments, looking for fires. I'm in short pants, ten years old, goddamn sixth grade. And all of a sudden I feel a hand on my leg. Hot and sweaty hand. I didn't know what to do."

"Go on."

"Dusty told me never to let anybody touch me like that. Didn't say why, just said don't. Well, I figure these guys are rangers, neighbors. Maybe they're just being friendly. Then the hand goes up my pants!"

"Quiet down."

"Okay. I got scared. I let him feel me for a second, then I turned around and looked at them, the pair of them. I see them staring at me. The weird eyes. Me, ten years old."

"What did you do?"

"I lit out of there. I was running so fast I nearly fell off the tower. I missed a railing and almost went over. They laughed, I swear to God. They'd have liked to see me go over."

"That's horrible, Rupert."

"That's six years ago, and they're still up there, leaning over me, looking down."

"My God."

"I wonder what they're going to do to us, Owen."

"They're already doing it, Rupert."

"Yeah."

"Jesus, I hurt."

"I don't think we've got a chance, Owen. I think we're going to die here."

"We've always got a chance."

"Yeah. Who's going to help us?"

"Your sister maybe."

"Ruthie? Ruthie can't even help herself."

"She's strong, Rupert. She's intelligent. She knows about Robin, everything. She'll help us."

"I wouldn't count on it."

"Why not?"

"Owen, you talked to her. You know damn well that Ruthie's not all there."

"I thought she was."

"She puts on a good show."

"Listen. . . . The dog's stopped barking."

"Probably exhausted."

"Whisper."

"Ruthie will do anything for Alvin. Anything he tells her to do. She's in love with him."

"She was, Rupert. But all that's changed. She told me."

"You can't always believe her."

"I believe she's a good person."

"Owen, if she had to decide between you and herself, she'd save herself."

"And if it were her or you, Rupert?"

"She'd save herself. Why do you think she's still alive? Ruthie'll do anything to survive."

"I got through to her, Rupert. She listened. I know she'll try to help me if she can."

"*If* she can."

"Right."

"You know what he does to her, Owen? He puts her in solitary confinement. She's there now, I bet. Alvin's nuts about solitary because it's legal. He's got solitary cells on every floor. You know the one I found you in? That's Ruthie's. Special for her. I came in once last winter and that's where she was. Said she'd been locked up two weeks, nothing to read, write, nothing but a blanket and a bucket."

"She didn't tell me that."

"She covers for him. That time I could have let her out. She wouldn't let me. She was afraid of what he might do. You should hear some of the things she told me."

"Tell me."

"There goes the dog."

"Forget the dog. Tell me about Ruth."

"Alvin used to let the men fuck her."

Owen shuddered.

"He brainwashed her, see? When she first came in here she was tough, tough as nails. She loved to be free. But after a year here she didn't want to leave. He pumped her full of drugs. He kept her so she didn't know where she was or what she was doing most of the time. She was being tortured here, like we are. And the only person who could help her was Alvin. That's how he controls her."

"Rupert, she told me she wants to leave. She asked me to help her."

"I could have gotten her out, Owen. We had plenty of chances. She'd talk about it, but she wouldn't go. 'No,' she says, 'I'm not ready. I'm still sick.' "

"She may be our only hope, Rupert."

"Then we're sunk."

"You think he'll kill us?"

"Worse. I think he'll brainwash us. Like he did Ruthie."

"We're strong men, Rupert."

"How about those poor bastards upstairs? They were strong men when they got here. They've got jelly for brains now."

"It would take a whole lot to wash my brain, Rupert."

"What makes you so sure?"

"Because I've got something to hang on to, something to live for. I've got my little boy and I'm going to get him out of here. Nothing can make me change that. And I'm strong, Rupert. I can lift the rear end of a car."

"Yeah. Well, how's that helping you now?"

"It's helping, believe me. I'm keeping my wits. I think he expected me to be gone by now. Cracked, broken. But I'm not. And I'm not going to crack no matter what he does."

"But we don't know what he does, Owen. We know what we've seen and heard, but we don't know the main thing."

"What main thing?"

"He's got a room down here somewhere, a special room."

"The Bad Room. I know."

"It's as low as you can go, Owen. Nobody's the same after the Bad Room."

"So they say."

"I wonder what it is."

"Maybe it's nothing."

"Nothing?"

"Maybe it's just a scare. You know, the way they scare kids with a story about the boogeyman. Maybe *this* is the Bad Room."

"Here?" Rupert said, staring at the door.

"Listen to me, forget the dog. The things I've seen, the things that have happened to me, have all seemed pretty crude at the time. But when you think about it, they're not so crude. There's something going on. Alvin knows what he's doing. Everything that's happened is part of his plan. And it's not crude, it's subtle, psychological. And we've been cooperating with him."

"God, Owen, you're right."

"He could have killed us, but here we are."

"Right."

"And if we're still alive, then Robin's still alive."

"I just hope he's doing better than we are."

Owen closed his eyes tight. "Don't say things like that, okay?"

"Sorry. I wasn't thinking when I said it. He's okay."

"We're okay, too. We're alive, Rupert. We're not dying, I'm not bleeding to death. He's hurt us, but he hasn't tried to kill us. If he wanted us dead he'd let that dog in."

The Doberman's shadow danced in the light coming under the door. It was barking, running at the door, slamming into it and bouncing off.

"That dog's going to kill itself," said Rupert. "Why don't they shoot it?"

"Part of the plan. It's meant to scare us, not hurt us."

"It's scaring me, Owen."

"It's just a dog."

147

"Owen, it's a Doberman pinscher that's been trained to attack people. And it's blood-crazy."

"That's what you're supposed to be thinking."

"But it's true."

"Rupert, the door is locked and the dog can't get in to us. It can make all the noise it wants, it can go nuts out there and smash itself apart, but it can't hurt us."

"You're right, Owen. You know what you said before, about my answer for everything? Well, I got to tell you. Everybody's crazy: Alvin, Ruth, the guards, everybody upstairs, everybody, even me. I'm crazy too, in my own way. But you're not, Owen. You got the best head here and I'm ready to listen to anything you got to say. That dog's not getting in here."

Then someone opened the door.

The room filled with light. Owen rolled into the wall, hiding his face, his genitals, but exposing the back of his neck. Rupert rolled on top of him, screaming as the dog attacked, shielding Owen's body with his own. Rupert shouted and thrashed, then stopped suddenly as a shot was fired. The gunshot was deafening in the small windowless room. It was followed by four more, silver flashes on the shadowed walls. Owen felt Rupert's body go limp. He felt something sharp jab him in his buttock. Then darkness.

Chapter Eight

OWEN DREAMED he was in a hospital room, in bed. He was very tired and could not move. There was a thermometer in his mouth. A short, heavyset man wearing pajamas removed the thermometer and read it. The man was Owen's father. On the other side of the bed, his head barely above the mattress, was Robin. Robin was wearing pajamas. Owen's father passed Robin the thermometer and Robin read it and shook his head.

"Dead," said Robin.

Owen's father nodded and shrugged. He took Robin's hand and together they stepped through a large window and plunged—somehow Owen knew the number—thirty stories.

Owen couldn't move a muscle to stop them.

"Owen?"

Total darkness, a tingling sensation, mild nausea, a voice.

"Owen, open your eyes."

Owen did not want to open his eyes. He wanted to stay where he was, in darkness, in ignorance of everything around him. Owen wanted to give up, quit, sleep forever. The voice would not let him.

"Wake up, Owen."

Owen opened his eyes. Staring at him from a

few feet away was a man's face, lined, yellowed, topped by silver hair. Sunken cheekbones, dark bags under pale blue eyes, sallow skin with red blotches, thin purplish lips, eyebrows missing. Owen closed his eyes.

Alvin slapped Owen's face.

"Come on, Owen," he said. "Wake up."

Owen opened his eyes, hoping the face had gone away. It hadn't. It was there, a foot from Owen's, staring down at him. The director's face was a dozen colors, all of them horrible.

"Where am I?"

"Where do you think?"

Owen tried to think and couldn't.

"I don't know."

"You're in Mizpah, Owen. You're in the Bad Room."

Then it all came back, the whole unending nightmare. He remembered the door, the dog, then the darkness, the dream.

"What happened?"

"You and your friend were under restraint. One of our people played a terrible trick. You passed out. Luckily we got to you before the dog did."

"And my friend?"

"Rupert was not so lucky."

"Oh."

"It was Rupert's screaming that brought us."

"Where is he?"

"They're burying him now. A double funeral."

"Double?"

"The dog, Owen. We had to shoot the dog. Are you comfortable?"

"I can't feel anything."

"Can you move your legs?"

"No."

150

"Try."

"I'm trying. I can't."

"Your arms, hands?"

"No."

"Getting plenty of air?"

"Yes."

"I'm tightening your chest straps. Let me know when you're having difficulty breathing. . . ."

"Now."

"That better?"

Owen gasped.

"Better?"

"I can hardly breathe!"

"How about now?"

"I can breathe."

"There. My name is Alvin. You may call me 'doctor' if you like."

"You're not a doctor."

"I'm your doctor, Owen."

"No you're not. You're nobody's doctor. You're—"

Alvin plunked a rubber mask over Owen's mouth and nose. Owen jerked his head away, but Alvin pressed harder, smothering him. Owen choked, his eyes on Alvin's. When they began to close, Alvin removed the mask.

"I'm not here to argue with you, Owen. I'm here to help."

"Where's my son?" Owen gasped.

"You have no son. You have a delusion."

"Alvin, let us go . . . let us out of here."

"Impossible. You're part of the place now. One of the family."

"No we're not."

"Owen, you're very sick."

"No I'm not."

151

"Owen, I'm the doctor here. I've lived with sickness all my life. I know."

"I'm not crazy."

"There's a disease in these woods, these Pines. It's catching and you've caught it."

"What's it called?"

"It doesn't have a name. And there's no cure, only relief. We're going to relieve you of all the symptoms. We're going to help you to stop suffering."

"Alvin, listen to me—"

Alvin placed the mask over Owen's face.

"Are we going to argue?"

Owen closed his eyes. Alvin removed the mask.

"How do you feel, Owen? Mentally, I mean."

"I'm dizzy."

"Hallucinations? Delusions?"

"No."

"Depressed?"

"I don't know." Owen kept his eyes closed.

"Do you feel anxious? Panicky?"

"Yes."

"Do you know why you're in Mizpah?"

"My son is here."

"You're in Mizpah because you're mad, Owen. Do you know why you're in the Bad Room?"

"No."

"Because you've been bad, bad about your external deportment, Owen. That's what concerns us here. Mizpah is your home, your nest, and you insist on soiling it."

"This is not my home. I don't belong here."

"Of course you'd say that. Other doctors have people come to them and say 'I'm sick, I'm doing bad things, help me.' But not me, Owen. My patients all say 'I'm fine, I'm good, leave me alone.' I get it all the time, Owen. I'm used to it."

"Alvin, if you let us go . . . just let us go . . . I'll give you anything you want. I swear."

"I don't want anything, Owen. I have everything I want. And I'm not going to throw it all away. Like you did."

"What?"

"You had a family, didn't you? A wife and a child. But you decided it wasn't enough. You kicked them out, didn't you?"

"Chief Howzer told you that."

"Answer my question, Owen."

"I got a divorce."

"Divorce is a sin, Owen. Marriage is holy."

Owen glared.

"We're very religious here."

"I know."

"Some people might think a madhouse is no place for God. But they're wrong. Don't you agree?"

"Yes. No. I don't know."

"They're dead wrong, Owen. How is your vision now?"

Alvin moved a few feet away. He waved a finger.

"Can you focus?"

"Yes."

Alvin, wearing his long, white, clinical coat, put his hands in his pockets and nodded his head thoughtfully. Slowly the rest of the room sharpened into focus.

There was one steel door and no windows. The walls were a dark mud brown with a glossy surface, faded in places from the damp. Two naked light bulbs burned in the brown ceiling, shedding a pale sickly light on the banks of machinery that lined the walls. Dull steel panels were set with dials and gauges, green screens and flickering lights. Gleaming chrome coils of fine wires snaked from the walls to the machines, running along the baseboards and disappearing through the floor. The narrow chamber reeked of disinfectant, vomit, and the metallic odor of burnt electrodes. By the door was a row of small black steel bottles in an oaken rack. Owen's eyes fastened on the bottles.

"Oxygen," said Alvin. "Not for you, I'm afraid."

"What are you going to do?"

"Do you have a certain feeling of dread, Owen?"

"Yes."

"Good. You feel helpless, cut off, about to die?"

"Yes."

"You might die, Owen. It's happened. It's very rare, but it has happened. People have died. Right here in this room."

"Don't . . ."

"It could happen, Owen. If I were to make a mistake, for example. A simple mistake while you're out cold. You'd never wake up."

"Oh my God . . ."

"Tell me this, Owen: during the funeral, when you were up there in the attic, did you have similar feelings, things you're feeling now?"

"Yes."

"Have you ever had these feelings before?"

"What is this?"

"Answer the question, Owen."

"No, I've never felt this way before."

"It's more than simple fear, isn't it?"

"Yes."

"You're scared to death. If I were you, I'd be scared out of my mind."

"You're not me, Alvin."

"No."

"It's what you want, isn't it?" Owen closed his eyes. "You want me to go mad."

"I want to help you adjust."

"You want me out of the way so you can steal my child."

"I want to give you peace, Owen. Peace of mind." Alvin tapped his temple, nodded his head.

"I don't want peace of mind. I just want Robin back."

"Sorry, Owen. You gave him up years ago. You ran away."

"Never. I never gave him up. His mother moved away."

"If you want to rationalize, to lie, go ahead. But you're just fooling yourself. I say you ran away."

"I don't care what you think."

"But you care what your son thinks. Don't you?"

"He'll grow up; he'll understand."

"He'll understand that his father was a sinner and a fornicator. And that his mother didn't care."

"What?"

"She's gone all day, Owen. Your son is growing up with strangers."

"Robin told you that! Jesus . . ."

"He's very ill."

"Let us go. Jesus God, *let us go!*"

Alvin came close to Owen, bent over him, and put a syringe to his arm. Owen tried to speak, but his words died in his throat. He closed his eyes, waiting for blackness, but it did not come. When he looked, Alvin's back was to him. He was by a machine, a wooden case that looked like a very old radio. He pushed a switch and a red light came on. He looked at his watch, then at Owen.

"Better? Calmed down?"

"Alvin, what do you want with us?" Owen's voice was weak, a whisper. The drug was dulling everything—sight, sound, and mind.

"Shall I tell you?" Alvin looked at the machine. "Tubes," he said. "She takes a little while to warm up."

Dragging his right foot, Alvin came to Owen and put his hand on his heart. Nodding, he sat on the bench where Owen lay, his hand resting on Owen's chest. As he spoke he looked at the machine.

"My father was a very lonely man. His father was a minister, a widower, and my father grew up alone, as I did. Were you an only child, Owen?"

"No."

"Brothers?"

"A brother and a sister."

"Then you were not lonely as a boy."

"No."

"I was. And my father was. When he was twenty he married my mother. My mother's parents were both dead by then, and she was very rich. She inherited everything from her parents, including a company that made breakfast food. But my mother was not well, Owen. She was not completely sane."

Alvin walked to a wooden cabinet and returned holding a gleaming metal object that looked to Owen like a very complicated pair of scissors. He placed it gently on the pad beside Owen's head where it was out of view, and, glancing at the little instrument, Alvin continued his story.

"Alcoholic parents, fights, divorce. Her mother drowned in a bathtub and her father went out a window. Then the lawyers and the judges went to work on her. When she married my father they tried to have it annulled. When that failed they tried to have her proved insane. They almost did. But my father outsmarted them. In the end he had her and all her money.

"Mother was ill, but she wasn't crazy. She was extremely shy. She had no ego and a very low self-image. She couldn't talk, couldn't look anyone in the eye. Not my father, not me. So he had to get her out of Philadelphia.

"So he built Mizpah. There was no wall then, just the Pines; the Pines were wall enough. They had this huge house for themselves and the servants, and they never left it. People came here to work for them, stayed until they could no longer stand the isolation, and quit. When my mother had her spells, doctors and nurses were brought in. They came, they comforted her, and they left. My father had no friends, no one to talk to. He talked to God. Do you talk to God, Owen?"

"Yes."

"My mother's money was in trust. It was controlled by the Philadelphia lawyers. My parents trusted them and never interfered. Money was made available to them whenever they wanted it and they supposed that things would always go on that way. The estate was worth millions, Owen. The interest was enough to build a place like Mizpah every year if they'd wanted. But all they wanted was to be left alone. My father loved my mother, Owen, if you can believe that. He did not marry her for her money alone.

"My father dreamed of filling this place with his children. He'd come from a small family and he wanted a big one. So did she. Their problems began when my mother became pregnant—with me."

On the machine a green light flashed on. Alvin looked at his watch, felt Owen's heart. He limped to the machine, turned a dial, and returned. Alvin was smiling, his mind on his story. He patted Owen's head and sat down beside him. He took up the shiny instrument, held it to the light, and turned a small screw. Then, in one swift motion he pushed it against Owen's cheek and slipped its edges under Owen's right eyelid. Slowly twisting two screws, he opened Owen's eye as wide as it would go. From a drawer he took a stainless-steel box the size and shape of a pencil case and opened the lid so that Owen could not see inside.

"Pregnancy had an adverse effect on my mother. She was despondent, melancholy, depressed. She cried all the time, and twice she tried to take her life. Toward the end of her pregnancy she had to be restrained. Finally I was born.

"I was born right here, in her bedroom in the attic. I was healthy, normal. My mother was not. She had become catatonic. She never left her bed. And so, there were no more children. No little brothers and sisters for me. Just this place, the dogs, and the servants. My father blamed me for my mother's condition, and he never spoke to me except to reprimand.

"My mother loved me. I remember feeling a great peace at her bedside, and I spent many hours of the day with her. As a boy I read a lot. I was always reading books. I used to read books aloud to mother, and she understood every word. At least I thought she did. Have you read *War and Peace?*"

"Yes."

"Well, when I was ten years old I read *War and Peace* aloud to my mother. It took me a year. Mother slept a lot, but she never slept while I was reading. That's how I knew she liked it. I read her *Crime and Punishment* and *Gone with the Wind.* All out loud, Owen, word by word. They were wonderful times.

"My mother began to improve. When I was twelve she got out of bed. She began to wear dresses again. She began to take strolls in the woods with my father. We all had such great hopes for her. And then my father read an article about a new cure for people with my mother's symptoms. It was new and unproven, but a doctor in Philadelphia told my father it would work. It was called EST, electroshock therapy. For the first time in years my father had hope.

"The problem was that my father refused to bring mother to Philadelphia for the cure. He felt it would be too hard on her, just seeing the city again after so many years in these woods. And no doctor would come here, not at any price. EST was so new, so controversial, that it was seldom practiced outside of military and state hospitals. No one would come here and risk his reputation."

From the stainless-steel case Alvin took a long thin instrument with a sharp point at each end. As Owen stared, unable to close or even blink his right eye, Alvin bent forward and jabbed the fine point into Owen's cornea. There was no pain, but his eye filmed over with a thin layer of blood.

Smiling, Alvin wiped it away with cotton. He placed the instrument back in its case.

"My father's hopes for the new cure were high. He was sure she would respond. So he placed ads in newspapers in this country and around the world. He finally got a response, from Rome. There was a doctor there, an Italian doing psychiatric research, who agreed to bring the cure to mother, but at a very high price. It was extortion, but my father sent for him immediately.

"His name was Diamante, Dottore Roberto Diamante, and he had worked with the Nazis in one of their clinics. My father didn't care about that. Living out here, he barely was aware of the war. Diamante arrived one day with a suitcase and a steamer trunk. In the trunk was that machine over there. It's an electroshock generator, and it's very powerful. The problem was that Diamante didn't know how to use it. He had used insulin shock, hot shock, and cold shock, but never electricity. All he knew was what he'd read in books.

"He moved in with us, ate with us at mealtimes, spent hours with my mother. The treatments had to wait until electricity was brought in. I'd grown up with gas, kerosine, and candles, and I was very excited about the electricity. To me it meant radios, record players, a good reading light. To my father it was part of the cure, part of something that would give mother back to us as a healthy, sane woman.

"They wired the house for electricity. Diamante set up his machine right here in this room. On the day after Christmas he began his treatments."

Alvin paused, ran his hands over his face. His right hand was constricted, clawlike, drawn into a fist from which the stub of an index finger jutted awkwardly. He trembled, swaying slightly on the bench. Then he stopped trembling, took up his story.

"We knew something had gone wrong after the first week. Mother's screams rang through the house. She resisted the treatments and had to be brought here by the servants each morning. Diamante would have no nurses. He knew that anyone with some real medical experience might expose him. Father had so much hope in EST that he would not put a stop to it until it was too late. When he refused to let Diamante work on her, the man fled. He'd been paid most of his fees, and he ran when given the chance. We never saw or heard from him again."

Alvin held up another shiny instrument, which Owen recognized as a scalpel. Staring at its delicate razor-sharp blade as if he had never seen it before, Alvin lowered it to his own mangled palm and slowly ran it across his skin. He winced with pain and the scalpel fell to the floor. He frowned and returned to his story.

"Mother was totally mad, worse than we had ever known her. She was in constant anguish. I won't go into it; it's not pretty. We had to have nurses then and it was difficult to get anyone at all. We had to make do with women who were not really nurses, who just came here to make some money for a while. I used to tell them what I thought of them, and they hated me.

"Mother lived not quite six months after her last shock treatment. A nurse left mother alone in a room with an open window. It was one of the attic rooms. You know it, don't you?"

"Ruth's room."

"Exactly. We didn't have the bars up then. But

at the time we did not think of Mizpah as a madhouse. Mother jumped headfirst out the window and broke her neck on the flagstones. Her sad, tragic life finally came to an end. There was no more of her, Owen. I had no mother, no one to read to, and, of course, no friends.

"I was taught by private tutors until I was old enough to go to college. When I was seventeen I left Mizpah, and went to the University of Pennsylvania in Philadelphia. Father provided me with a car and my own apartment. He didn't think I was ready for a dormitory, and he was right. I was the loneliest I'd ever been. When I sat down to eat in the cafeteria I ate with hundreds of people and I ate alone. I had no idea how to talk to people my age, how to converse with women. I tried and I failed every time. They thought I was strange and they made jokes about me to my face. So I sat in the back of my classes and I lived alone, cut off from everyone.

"I studied psychology. I wanted to know why people acted the way they did. I thought I could help myself and that I could someday help others. I wanted to enter a field where I lived and worked with many people, people who needed me. I dreamed that we would all get better together, you see?"

"Yes."

"Am I boring you, Owen?"

"No."

"I'll stop if you like." Alvin looked at his watch. "We have a lot to get through."

"No, please go on."

"I had a year to go before graduation. I was determined to get my degree, go to graduate school,

162

get my doctorate. But that summer everything changed. My father went broke.

"It was the lawyers, Owen. The lawyers and the courts. They were in league with certain distant members of my mother's family. They used my mother's suicide to prove that she was a maniac and always had been. Father was about to lose everything—the house, grounds, income, everything. He was forced to settle out of court. He was left with Mizpah and a few thousand dollars.

"Father had a plan, and for the first time in my life he began talking to me. The house was huge. With the servants gone it was even bigger, emptier. Father thought it would make an ideal rest home for old people. He borrowed some money, hired a staff, and advertised. In a few weeks we had dozens of applications. We opened that fall.

"I never went back to school. I stayed right here. I found that in three years at college I'd picked up quite a bit of psychology. I'd had a course in geriatrics and here I was with a houseful of patients. My father and I were getting along, working together, and we worked very hard. Mizpah was a good place then, Owen. It was benign.

"We prospered, and when we made some money we put it back into the place, made it clean and comfortable for our guests. Everything out back was green lawn, right up to the Pines. We had a doctor and four nurses in residence, and I was in charge of recreation and other therapies. I studied quite a bit of therapy at school, you know, and it was exciting to be able to try out different techniques on real people. Some of our guests were quite ill, though not all of them knew it. I took the hardest cases, Owen, the toughest. I had a lot of success.

"Everything would have gone well if it hadn't been for the blabbermouths. You know that mental health is a very touchy business. Especially with therapy. Many of the things I was doing were new, experimental, unorthodox. They were not always pleasant. Do you know what I'm talking about, Owen?"

"No."

"You're probably thinking that I was fooling around with EST, with mother's machine. Right?"

"Yes."

"Well, you're wrong. That came later. I wouldn't have touched that machine for a million dollars. It sat down here, right in that corner, and it collected dust."

Alvin glared at the machine like an angry child.

"What did you give me, Alvin?"

"Atropine. It's a muscle paralyzer. How do you feel?"

"I don't feel anything."

"Can you move your legs? Here, I'll undo your leg straps. How's that?"

"I can't move."

"Try your fingers."

Owen's fingers moved sluggishly.

"It takes a little while to set in. Breathing okay?"

"Yes."

Alvin went to the corner where the machine hummed, the red light glowed. Owen could barely turn his head to watch. Alvin limped back to Owen's side carrying a handful of small metal plates with wires attached to them. The wires, thin and insulated with clear plastic, were connected to another machine.

164

"No!" begged Owen, turning his head to one side. It was his only defense, his only possible movement.

"Relax, Owen. They're only sensors. Electrocardiograph, electroencephalograph. We're going to monitor your heart and your brain, okay?"

Owen shook his head.

"If you're not going to cooperate I'll just give you some more atropine. There's a risk."

Owen lay still, his eyes on Alvin. Sensors were placed on his forehead and fixed there with tape.

"Move your fingers."

Owen tried and could not move them. Alvin released the straps that bound Owen's arms and chest. Owen could feel nothing and no part of his body would obey his mind. He could move his head slightly, he could move his eyes. The rest of him was totally paralyzed. Alvin taped sensors to Owen's chest. Carefully he led the wires to the gray machine and attached them, reading the dials. He returned to his perch on the bench, beside Owen.

"How's that?"

"I . . . I . . . I . . ."

"You're having difficulty speaking. Don't try. Just listen, all right? Can you hear me?"

"Y . . . yes."

"You feel nothing?"

"Nothing." Owen's voice was flat, dead.

"Good. Now, where were we? Therapies, that's it. You know something, Owen? To me everything is therapy. Waking, rising, eating, walking, working, having fun, making love, making plans—it's all therapy. And, of course, in a situation like Mizpah's the best therapy is carried out in groups. My groups were set up to suit guest needs, and every guest had to be a member of a group. Some of them didn't want to be grouped, for example. So they were put into a group that didn't want to be a group, and that becomes therapy, you see?"

"I . . . I don't know."

"It doesn't matter. But you can imagine that certain of our guests, those with large imaginations, were sometimes displeased with what they saw or heard. These were our blabbermouths, and we didn't realize it, but they were working against us. They were telling their relatives terrible things about us, all exaggerations and lies of course, but very damaging to our reputation. We began to lose guests and fewer were coming in."

Alvin stared at Owen's face. With a jerky movement he unscrewed the surgical device from Owen's eye and flung it across the room, blinking as it bounced off the wall. He rubbed his face, took a deep breath, and went on.

"No guests, no money, Owen. It's as simple as that. The money was short and running out. Father said we had to make cuts. We made them, but things just got worse. Our doctor left us and we replaced our nurses with local women, not all of whom were competent. We saw abuses going on, but we were powerless to stop them. Then, suddenly, we found ourselves under investigation.

"The list of violations was endless. They accused us of things we didn't even know about. Father and I were frantic with worry and brokenhearted that all our efforts were bringing us only trouble and guilt. We were down to half a dozen guests when the State closed us down."

Alvin limped to a small table and returned with a syringe. Owen felt nothing as the needle sank into his arm. He waited, terrified, for its effect.

166

"Just speeding up your heart a little, okay? Feel any different?"

"No."

"Mind racing? Thoughts bouncing like Ping-Pong balls?"

"Yes."

"Your EEG's going crazy. You must feel terrible."

"I . . . can't . . . stop . . ."

"Don't try. It should pass in a while." Alvin paused for a moment, trying to remember where he had left off.

"Well, they closed us down and here we were, father and I, all alone. But father was a tough man, Owen. Nothing could keep him down. In the years he had been living here as a rich and retired gentleman, he had made some important contacts with the local authorities. Now, as you know, the politicians of this State are probably the most corrupt in the country. You can get anything you want out here, if you have the money. So father bought influence, and influence made Mizpah part of the state mental hospital system, albeit a very small, remote, and insignificant part. Money from the State opened our doors and put us on our feet again. Of course, the nature of the place was changed drastically.

"We were no longer a rest home, Owen. We had become a lunatic asylum in one of the most overcrowded mental hospital systems in the country. Conditions in many places were comparable to concentration camps. And Mizpah, I'm afraid to say, was quickly thrust into the pattern. We were officially equipped to handle fifty patients, Owen. We were sent one hundred and eighty. The ward personnel they sent us weren't trained, and controlling so many patients often made them frustrated and brutal. And the worst of it was that more patients were coming in than going out.

"The psychiatrists they sent us were fools. Their theory was that most of the patients had degenerative diseases and there was little that could be done to help them or even keep them alive. People were dying from lack of care. And they were dying from other things. A lot of physically damaging methods were justified simply because they forced patients to conform to institutional life.

"Not that any of this was new. But what happened was technology. When the State took us over, they were using shock everywhere. I read up on it and found out many intriguing things. It's not called electroshock therapy anymore. It's called electro*convulsive* therapy, ECT. I found out that with certain modifications, mother's machine was equipped to do anything a modern generator can do. Am I getting too technical?"

"W . . . what are you . . . doing to me?"

"I haven't done it yet."

"Please . . ."

"It's the atropine, Owen. Combined with the stimulant it induces a certain panic. I could combat that with barbiturates, but I won't. I could erase your consciousness with a good general anesthetic, but that would defeat the therapy, wouldn't it? You're not going to miss a minute of this, Owen. That's essential."

"Oh . . . my . . . God."

"Nothing can help you, Owen. God's not allowed in the Bad Room."

". . . torture . . ."

"Therapy. Remember, everything's therapy.

168

This is your therapy. It is also mine. It works both ways."

"S . . . stop."

"I didn't know much about electricity, Owen, but what I learned I put to use. I gave mother's machine a good going over, and then I began to work with it. My first patients were dogs. I understand the puppy is yours."

"I . . . can't . . . t . . . talk."

"Stop trying. It's not worth the effort. The puppy likes us, Owen. It likes it here. So will you. We haven't much here, I admit. But it's better than outside, better than the Pines. My father hated the Pines. They brought him terrible luck all his life. He died. His funeral was the first Mizpah funeral the patients were allowed to witness. His funeral started them all.

"Owen, a man can only try so hard, do so much. The State made it quite clear to me that Mizpah would always be a back ward. We would house and handle the very worst cases, the incurables, the dangerous ones. As things grew worse I leaned more and more heavily on the only woman I have ever loved . . . Ruth Sooey. With Ruth I could cope, I could endure. I loved her and she loved me and I was strong, healthy, young. Then something happened that changed all that. I want to tell you about it, Owen, because it's the last part of the picture, the part that's hardest to look at."

Alvin's eyes traveled from one machine to another in quick, darting glances. He coughed, covered his mouth, then stared at his hand. His wrist jerked, upsetting the stainless-steel box, which clattered to the floor. Alvin seemed not to notice.

"They buried me alive out there, Owen. I was one hour in the ground. Nailed into a box and under six feet of soil with madmen dancing on my grave. Can you imagine that? *Can you?* ANSWER ME!"

"No."

"Well, I want you to try, Owen. You think you're helpless on this table? Think about being buried out there, buried in a box so narrow your arms can barely move. You know there's no way out, but you try anyway. You scratch wood until your nails tear off from the roots, then you go on clawing. You push, push against a ton of earth until your bones snap and your sinews tear. It's dark, Owen, pitch black, and all you can hear is the thuds and thumps of the idiots above you, the men you tried to help. And gradually you lose something, you give something up. Something leaves you and stays there in the ground, even after they dig you up, even after the guards breathe life back into you, after the sun shines in your eyes and you know you're alive; even then, Owen, you know something is gone, it's down there in that hole, in that box, in that . . . that . . ."

Alvin was panting, trembling. He looked at his hands, the torn, stunted fingers, the mangled joints, ripped tendons. He put his hands in his pockets and smiled.

"You can't imagine it, Owen, not until you've experienced it. And that's what we're here for. We're going to bury you, Owen. We're going to simulate everything I went through, and when we're done we'll be friends, you see? We'll have so much in common—"

"No!"

"And Ruth. Ruth's going to see things our way, Owen. Ruth's going to be here always, because she's going to be a mother. And not just a mother

170

to our little Robin. She'll be my mother and your mother, too. And believe me, Owen, when we're through here, a mother is all you'll ever want."

"LET ME GOOOOOOOO!"

Alvin leaned over Owen and stared hard into his face. Shaking his head, his mouth set, he went to the machine and picked up two black steel rods, which were attached to the machine by thick wires; sponges were taped to the ends. Alvin turned a dial and pressed a switch. He limped back to Owen and stood behind him, a rod held carefully in either hand.

"I've never done this unassisted," he said.

Owen rolled his head to one side. Alvin put the electrodes on the bench and straightened Owen's head.

"Owen, listen to me. I don't want to kill you. You're ill and I'm here to help. It's your brain, Owen. We don't want to fry it."

"Aaaaaagh . . ."

Quickly Alvin plunged a rubber sponge into Owen's open mouth, thrusting the gag deep into his throat.

"Brain cells that are sick, and cells that are potentially sick, have to be destroyed."

Owen's eyes opened wide.

"The most important thing is to make sure that every cell that is affected is completely burnt."

Owen watched as the heavy black electrodes in Alvin's hands came closer, closer.

"We're nailing down the lid, Owen. We're lowering you into the hole."

The explosion in Owen's brain was followed by total darkness.

Chapter Nine

FOR WHAT seemed like hours Owen's tortured mind was a total blank. Then he heard a voice.

"You moved your head."

"Huh?"

"Grand mal."

"What?"

"How do you feel?"

"Okay."

"Do you know who you are?"

"Sure."

"What's your name?"

"Owen . . . Vanderbes."

"Do you know where you are?"

"Ha! That I'm not so sure about."

"Look around you. Do you remember this room?"

"Nope. Some kind of hospital?"

"Do you remember me?"

"Sorry."

"You're in a mental hospital. My name is Dr. Alvin."

"Ah."

"Remember now?"

"A little. What happened?"

"You just went through a grand mal convulsion induced by electric shock."

"I did?"

"You can't remember it?"

"Not a thing, doc."

"It's temporary. There's always memory loss with a grand mal."

"What's that?"

"French, Owen. You got a 'big bad' convulsion. As opposed to a 'little bad' one, a petit mal. You wouldn't forget a petit mal."

"Oh."

"Do you feel sad? Depressed?"

"Not at all, doctor. I feel fine."

"Do you know why you're here?"

Owen tried to shake his head and gave up. "No," he said.

"Try to lift your arm."

"Can't budge it."

"Legs?"

"Nope."

"If you begin to feel things in any part of your body, will you let me know?"

"Certainly, doctor."

"I need help," said Alvin. He looked at his watch.

"Anything I can do?"

"What? No, no. It's all right."

"Boy, it's really something."

"What is?"

"How I feel. I mean I feel much better."

"Better than before?"

"Absolutely."

"Do you remember how you felt before?"

"Bad."

"Do you remember why you felt so bad?"

"Uh-uh."

"Not a thing?"

"Nope."

"Shall I tell you?"

"What?"

"What's wrong with you."

"Please do, doctor."

"You're being treated for S-type depression. That's endogenous, somatic depression."

"Is that bad?"

"It's the worst. You're lucky though, because ECT has its best results with S-type."

"ECT?"

"Electroconvulsive therapy. Got it?"

"Got it."

"Modified."

"Modified?"

"Atropine and oxygen. I had to breathe you."

"I can't remember."

"See if you can follow me, Owen. I just delivered an electric shock across your brain. The shock caused your body to convulse for nearly seven minutes. For a part of that time you stopped breathing and were force-ventilated. Got that?"

"I think so."

"It's not important. The convulsion is secondary. The big kick is the brain seizure. The convulsion in the body is paralleled by a cerebral seizure. It's the seizure that produces the results."

"Ah. I got it."

"You had a tremendous seizure, Owen. The first one is always that way."

"I'm getting more?"

"You're getting more shocks; no more seizures. Not if I can help it."

"Okay."

"When you moved your head you doubled the duration. More than doubled it. You went eighty

percent over your convulsion threshold. You had a
classic. Only it wasn't what we wanted."

"No?"

"No. The goal is petit mal."

"Right."

"No harm done. We'll just try again."

"I'm ready."

"You are?"

"Sure. Go ahead."

"Will you try to remain still?"

"I'll try, doc."

"We both have to work at this, you see."

"I see."

"See that point on the ceiling?"

"Where?"

"That. That sort of stain."

"I see it."

"Stare at that. Keep your head absolutely
still."

"I can do it, doctor. Once I set my mind to
something—"

"No more talking now."

Alvin made some adjustments on the machine,
frowning at the dials and gauges. Then, taking his
position behind Owen's head, he picked up the two
slim electrodes and leaned forward. Owen smiled
as they came nearer.

The lightning bolt that crashed through Owen's
brain was followed by a sort of rolling thunderlike
sound.

"Sorry, Owen," Alvin said.

"Wha?"

"Grand mal."

"Granma?"

"Owen?"

"Wha."

"You convulsed again."

"Waz thad?"

"Owen, say your name."

"Owa . . ."

"Say 'Owen Vanderbes.'"

"Owa . . . wanarzz."

"Count to three."

"Wad . . . dob . . . fru . . ."

"Dysarthria. The way you're talking. It's a postconvulsive speech impairment. It goes away. How do you feel?"

"Agh."

Alvin prepared a hypodermic and put it into Owen's arm. He waited, his eyes on the machine. Owen's breathing became more rapid.

"Your head clearing?"

"Yes."

"Lidocaine. You remember anything?"

"Yes. You're Dr. Alvin. I'm in a mental—"

"I mean anything about the seizure. Do you have any recollection at all of what you've just been through?"

"Drowning. It was like I was drowning."

"Well, you were. You didn't breathe throughout the tonic stage of the convulsion. About ninety seconds."

"Oh."

"You lost a few cells on that one, Owen."

"Is that good?"

"Sure is. What we're doing, Owen, is we're sacrificing a few pieces to win the game."

"I see."

"Brain damage and reduced mental functions are good for some mental patients. Patients like you."

"Like me, doctor?"

176

"Some patients simply have more intelligence than they can handle. Do you see?"

"I think so."

"We put a few groups of cerebral neurons out of service and we begin to get somewhere. But I'm afraid we've got a long way to go before we have a real dysfunction. And we're not going to get it through oxygen deprivation, either."

"No?"

"Too tricky. The apnea shortens with each convulsion. You just got another convulsion that you never should have had."

"Was it my fault, doctor?"

"It was mine. But I've never done this alone. There have to be two of us: one on the machine, one on you."

"I get it."

"Owen, do you remember coming to Mizpah?"

"Mizpah?"

"Here. The mental hospital."

"No. Not really. I mean when I try to remember, I forget."

"Does that frighten you?"

"Some."

"Do you remember anyone else you met here?"

"No."

"No one?"

"My mind's a blank."

"Postseizure confusion. It goes away."

"I'll remember everything?"

"You'll remember anything you like."

"Good."

"But the things you thought were so important just won't matter very much. Not when we're all through. But we're going to have to stop these convulsions. They're not getting us anywhere."

177

"Oops."

"What? What was that, Owen?"

"My arm moved."

"It jerked? Of its own accord?"

"No, I moved it. I think."

"Try it again."

Owen tried. His arm raised a few inches above his chest. The effort tired him and he let it drop.

"I'll take care of that," said Alvin. He gave Owen another injection, his eyes on the oscillographs that recorded Owen's heartbeat and brain waves.

"Try again."

Owen was immobile.

"Shake your head."

He couldn't do it.

"Owen? Repeat my name."

Silence.

"Say anything at all."

Nothing.

"Can you blink your eyes?"

He couldn't do it.

"You're totally paralyzed. But you're wide awake, eh? I know that because I'm looking at your brain waves. You're slowing, but you're reacting. Let's see what we can do."

Alvin filled a syringe, injected it into Owen's thigh. He checked his watch.

Owen moaned.

"Speak. Say something."

"I . . . don't like it, doctor."

"Say it again."

"I don't like it."

"What? What don't you like, Owen?"

"The way I feel."

"Do you feel like crying?"

"I am crying."

"No you're not. Do you feel pain?"

"No . . . not really."

"What do you feel?"

"Like I'm dying."

"A part of you is dying."

"Oh my God."

"You're showing severe brain-wave pathology."

"Oh God."

"It passes."

"Please. Please let it pass."

"That last shot was succinylcholine. It modifies the atropine. In a minute you'll be fine."

Together they waited a minute, two minutes, in silence. Then, "Doctor?"

"Yes?"

"I . . . can I go home?"

"Where is home?"

"Sea . . . bright."

"No. Not anymore."

"No?"

"No. Your home is Mizpah. Say 'Mizpah.' "

"Mizpah."

"Mizpah what?"

"Mizpah . . . benediction."

"No, Owen. Mizpah lunatic asylum."

"Mizpah . . . lunatic . . . lunatic?"

"That's real good, Owen."

"Doctor?"

"Yes."

"But can I go home someday? To my real home?"

"Never. That's all over, Owen. You're here for good."

"Why?"

"Well, you became ill. And in the course of your illness you became violent."

"Did I hurt someone?"

"I'm afraid so."

"Who?"

"Your family, Owen. Do you remember them?"

"I . . . no."

"You had a wife and child, Owen. Don't you remember?"

". . . a little."

"They loved you, Owen. Even when you got sick. They stuck by you. But you killed them both."

"Oh no."

"Someone else might have gone to the electric chair, Owen. The electric chair."

"Oh Jesus."

"But not you. You were found innocent by reason of insanity. You won't be executed, Owen. But, of course, you can never leave us."

"But I don't like it here."

"It's the succinylcholine. A side effect. You're having an extreme anxiety-depression reaction. It will wear off."

"I don't like it at all."

"You're not supposed to."

"God, I want to die. I feel awful."

"Nausea?"

"Yes, everything. I feel horrible. My own wife and child?"

"And your dog. You killed your pet dog, too."

"I . . . I just feel terrible, doctor."

"Okay. Okay, Owen, I'm going to do something I didn't plan on doing. It'll set us back a bit, but it's necessary. You're getting a general anesthetic, sodium pentothol. You're going out and

180

when you're back we'll start again. We're not going to get anywhere until we have missed-seizure, and for that I'll need help."

Alvin pushed a syringe into Owen's hip and started for the door.

"Where are you going?"

"To get my assistant. I'll be right back."

"Don't leave me, doctor."

"I'll be right back."

"Please don't go."

"You won't even know I'm gone. You should black out in about five more seconds."

"Doctor, please . . ."

Alvin unlocked the door, opened it. He looked back and frowned.

"Owen . . . you're about to undergo quite a bit of anguish, mental and physical. You're going to know pain that few have ever experienced outside of this room."

"Doctor, I beg you . . ."

Alvin smiled. "Are you going to be a baby?"

"He's coming around, Alvin."

"Yes. I see his heart rate."

"I see his eyes. Owen?"

"He can't speak, Ruth."

"Owen, it's me: Ruth Sooey."

"He can't say a word, Ruth. He's catatonic."

"But he's looking right at me."

"Believe me, he doesn't know who you are."

"What happened to him?"

"He snapped, Ruth. He went over the edge."

"Why?"

"It was something he saw. It unhinged him."

"What?"

181

"He saw the funeral this morning. They buried a dog. He thought they were burying his boy."

"Oh no."

"I'm afraid so."

"What are you going to do?"

"With your help, Ruth, I'm going to treat him."

"For what?"

"Dementia praecox."

"Are you sure, Alvin?"

"Dementia paratonita, paratonia progressiva, amblynoia simplex, dysphrenia, schizophrenia . . . call it what you like. He shows every classic symptom."

"But look at his eyes, Alvin. He looks like he's pleading with me, begging."

"Paranoia."

"He can't move a muscle?"

"He's akinetic. Chronic lack of willpower. He's living in what's called a hysteriform twilight state. The paranoia lacks any real basis."

"But his son's been kidnapped, Alvin. I know he's worried about his little boy."

"He may have been. Not now."

"Alvin, look at his eyes! I mentioned his boy and—"

"Schizophrenic depression. Anxiety, panic—simple, painful emotions and feelings independent of events. It's abstract melancholia."

"He looks at me, not you, Alvin. See?"

"Manic withdrawal. Remember, he's hallucinating."

"He seemed like such a strong man."

"He never touched you?"

"Of course not."

"And you'd never seen him before?"

"Never. We've been through that all last night, Alvin."

"If I thought there were something between you two I wouldn't waste my time on him."

"Alvin, will you stop? What's that?"

"Electroencephalogram. You're looking at his brain waves, Ruth."

"They're jerky."

"Akinetic catatonia. That's the pattern. He's passively registering everything that goes on about him, but it's doubtful if he's doing any real thinking."

"Look at the needle bounce!"

"Faxen-psychosis. Ganser syndrome. Spin-off of the catatonia."

"He doesn't understand a word we're saying?"

"Ruth, he's totally confused. Delusions, waking dreams, constant psychic trauma. What we call Benommenheit. It's an internal fugue state. Nothing connects."

"Is he suffering?"

"Terribly."

"Can't we comfort him somehow?"

"We're going to try, Ruth, but I'll need your help. Ordinarily I use Cebulski, but he's not to be trusted anymore."

"Where is he?"

"Isolation. When he's softened up we'll bring him down here for the same treatment."

"What is the treatment, Alvin? What do you do down here?"

"Nothing very exciting, nothing new. All I really know about it is that it works. Most of the time."

"What? What works?"

"It's all above your head, Ruth."

183

"Tell me what you do."

"All right, let's see. Imagine that the human mind is like an anthill. Not an ordinary anthill, but one of those that's set between two pieces of glass so that we can see everything that goes on.

"Now then, Owen's anthill is very old. It's been building for over thirty years, right? It has tunnels and chambers and all the things that ants have. It's very complex, but very ordered. Every ant knows what to do. The queen ant and the worker ant and the anthill are all one, you see."

"Okay."

"Okay, but then, after Owen's thirty or so years, something goes wrong. Some of the ants start acting differently, hurting other ants, destroying the anthill. We don't know which ants are doing what, only that some of them are misbehaving. Well, what we do is we shake up the anthill, with that machine over there. It uses electricity to give the patient's brain a good shake."

"I've read about shock therapy."

"Well, this isn't quite that. This is my modification, my refinement, Ruth. When we're finished there won't be an anthill, just sand and ants. The healthy ones build a new hill. The rest will be dead."

"What do I have to do?"

"Take these electrodes, one in either hand, and place them here and here."

"Like this?"

"Exactly."

"Alvin, look at his eyes. He looks terrified."

"It has nothing to do with us."

"What are these marks on his forehead?"

"Where?"

"Here and here. They're burns, Alvin."

184

"It's nothing serious. I was attempting to treat him when he moved his head."

"But he can't move."

"It was an opisthotonos jerk due to shock. That's how I lost control."

"But what if he moves again?"

"It won't matter."

"It won't?"

"No, because duration will be controlled by the machine, not by your hands. With the electrodes in place I merely have to push this switch. The machine is set at a tenth of a second, on a low, subconvulsive current."

"What's that mean?"

"We're not going to convulse him. There will be no brain seizure. There will be what we call a missed-seizure. It's a technique I've been working on for years."

"It's so technical, Alvin. Do you know what you're doing?"

"Watch."

Owen's body arched, then went limp.

"Jesus, Alvin!"

"Excellent."

"Alvin, look at his eyes."

"Glazed over. It'll pass."

"Is it painful, Alvin?"

"Not at all."

"But his eyes . . . he looks like he's in terrible pain. Can I take away the electrodes?"

"No. He's getting another."

"He moved!"

"An involuntary jerk. Central nervous system, not the brain."

"I think he's had enough."

"I'll decide that, Ruth. Ready?"

"Another?"

"Yes. Hold on."

"Wait! Look at the encephalograph, Alvin. Look at his brain waves."

"I'm looking. Watch."

"Alvin! The needle almost went off the chart!"

"Petit mal."

"His eyes are closed, Alvin."

"We'll give him a rest."

"He looks dead!"

"Look. Look here at his heart rate. He's quite alive, Ruth."

"What do I do with the electrodes?"

"Put them down. Calm yourself."

"I'm a wreck."

"Sit down. You'll stop trembling."

"It's horrible."

"It doesn't look pleasant. But believe me, it's benign. See now, he's resting. One by one we are relieving him of his torments."

"Are you sure?"

"Of course."

"Alvin, look at his lips. They're moving."

"It's a tic, nothing more."

"No. He's trying to say something. Owen?"

"Sit down, Ruth."

"What are you doing?"

"I'm going to give him an injection."

"What are you giving him?"

"Just a tranquilizer. I want to slow his heart. . . . *There.*"

"His mouth's stopped."

"It was just a tic."

"It looked like he was trying to form words."

"If he could I'm sure they wouldn't interest you."

"His eyes are open. Look."

"I see."

"They're clearer."

"He's ready."

"For what?"

"For treatment, Ruth. We're continuing."

"Alvin, please, he's had enough. He looks like he's in agony."

"Ruth, this is multiple missed-seizure. It's the only way it works. Apply the electrodes, please."

"Couldn't we wait a little bit?"

"We've got a lot to get through, Ruth."

"A lot? How many shocks will he get?"

"Oh, forty or fifty."

"Alvin! Look at his eyes!"

Alvin shrugged and turned back to his instruments. But Ruth, unable to tear her eyes from Owen's stare, read the pain and terror that surfaced from deep within his mind.

"Alvin, I'm afraid."

"Afraid? Of what?"

"Look at his cardiogram. When you press that button his heart stops."

"It slows, it doesn't stop."

"Could he die?"

"Oh, we could kill him if we wanted to. A hundred milliamperes delivered across the brain stem would be fatal."

She put down the electrodes. As she did so Owen opened his eyes and looked at her. His eyes were red, bloodshot, and dry.

"Why are you stopping?"

"I . . . I'm tired, Alvin. Let me rest."

"All right. Take a moment. We'll let the machine cool down a bit."

"How many has he had?"

"Six, seven."

"You don't know how many?"

"I haven't been counting."

Ruth put her hand on Owen's forehead.

"He's hot, Alvin. Like a fever."

"Feel his chest."

"It's cool."

"His frontal lobes are taking the brunt of the damage."

"What damage?"

"Petechial hemorrhages; subarachnoid hemorrhages."

"What's that?"

"Brain pathology, Ruth. It's the essence of the therapy."

"He'll be able to move again, walk, talk?"

"That's the object."

"Will it change him?"

"Naturally."

"To what?"

"He'll be one of our inmates, Ruth. He'll fit right in upstairs."

As Ruth paced around the room she kept her eyes on Owen. She noticed that his eyes followed her wherever she moved.

"He has such intelligent eyes, Alvin. So sensitive."

"That's in your head, Ruth."

"No. I saw his eyes last night. They have the same look. Will he be an idiot?"

"He'll have losses in certain areas."

"What areas?"

"Oh, abstract reasoning, judgment, insight. But he won't be needing those things anymore, you see. They have to go if we're to get to the real root of his neurosis."

188

"It seems such a shame."

"Are you rested?"

"No."

"Come. Come sit by me. I'll hold you."

"I'm all right, Alvin. You look exhausted. You should sleep."

"Not until we're through."

"How do you know when he's had enough?"

"We'll know from his eyes. When they've lost that haunted look we'll stop."

"He never stops looking at me."

"You're a meaningless blur, Ruth. I'm sure."

Ruth bent over Owen and looked closely at his face. Tears had formed in the corners of his eyes, and one was rolling down his cheek. Ruth dabbed it with a corner of the sheet.

"What are you doing to him, Ruth?"

"Nothing."

"Don't touch him."

"I was just cleaning his face."

"We'll get him cleaned up later."

"I feel better now."

"Okay. Let's continue."

"I'm all set."

"Fine. We're going to slow the pulse for this series."

"What's that do?"

"It draws it out, prolongs it."

"I see."

"Apply the electrodes. I'll count the shocks this time, Ruth."

"Go ahead."

"One."

"He got it."

"How are his eyes, Ruth?"

Owen's eyes were clear, dry, looking directly into Ruth's.

"Getting vague, Alvin."

"Two."

"It's working now, I'm sure."

"Three."

"I'm with you, Owen."

"Don't talk to him."

"Okay."

"Four."

"Got it."

"I'm not getting brain jerks. Are you sure you have good contact, Ruth?"

"I'm doing it just the way you showed me."

"Press down."

Ruth held the electrodes a fraction of an inch away from Owen's skin and pretended to press down.

"Go," she said.

"Five."

Ruth looked into Owen's eyes and winked.

Owen, with unspeakable pain and infinite labor, closed one eyelid and winked back.

Chapter Ten

NOTHING HAPPENED.

"Odd," said Alvin.

"What's wrong?"

"He's not reacting."

Owen's eyes were closed. He was resting, praying, hoping that Ruth would act.

"Alvin, he's not . . ."

"Oh, he's alive, Ruth. Physically he's still with us. But mentally . . . well, his brain's showing no reaction to the charge. None at all."

"He's had too much."

"He has not."

"How can you be sure?"

"You know little Patruzi upstairs?"

"Yes?"

"He's had forty at one go. At *least* forty. Welter went through ninety missed-seizures in three days."

"But they're not even human anymore."

"They're happy."

"Happy? Alvin, an idiot can't be happy or sad."

"You're very wrong, Ruth. I know that both those men are better off now than when they were . . . than before their therapy. You don't remember Welter then. He was incorrigible. Patruzi

191

wept from morning to night. And both of them were *bad.*"

"This man's done nothing wrong."

"Are you going to argue with me? Because if you are, I'll put you back in that cell and have Mahoney help me. He'd be only too glad to."

Ruth looked down at Owen, said nothing. In her hands the twin electrodes were poised like pencils over Owen's temples.

"I'm stepping up the voltage, Ruth. Ready?"

Owen's eyes were slitted, focused on the rods. He was a helpless object at the mercy of the frightened woman and the psychotic "doctor." Either the blinding, white-hot horror would once again pass over him, or it would not. There was nothing he could do but wait.

Ruth, steadying her hands, held the electrodes far enough from Owen's flesh that there could be no chance of contact.

"Ready," she said.

There was a pause, a silence while Alvin pressed the button, regarding the twin meters.

"Very odd," he said.

"Alvin, let's stop."

"No."

"But you need rest. You're worn out, exhausted. Please, can't we stop?"

"Ruth, we are not stopping."

"But why, Alvin? Why can't it wait?"

"Because I've waited long enough! Wonderful things are happening now, Ruth, things that will change our lives, give us what we always wanted. And this man is standing in the way."

"How?"

"Prepare the electrodes. Press down."

Ruth pretended to do as she was told.

"God damn it, something's wrong," Alvin said.

"Maybe the machine's broken."

"No. It's delivering current."

"Alvin, I want to know what this has to do with us, with our future."

"Are you pressing down?"

"Yes!"

"It's simply not getting through. All right, I'm going to go for forty joules, and by God that's enough to boil water. Get ready."

"Alvin, I want to stop this."

Alvin looked at her, his eyes wide, his forehead wrinkled. A cruel smile played on his lips. His face twitched with the distortion of a manic tic. Then his voice boomed, "God damn it, Ruth, we're not stopping until this man's brain is a scrambled egg!"

Ruth recoiled, inhaled deeply, then composed herself and replied, "Yes, Alvin."

"That's understood?"

"Yes."

"Just remember: this could be happening to you."

"I know."

"No more objections?"

"No more."

"I'm going to check the fuses, then we'll begin again." Alvin pulled the machine away from the wall and bent over it, his back to Ruth. Ruth looked at Owen and nodded solemnly. Owen winked both eyes. He watched Ruth scan the room, then walk softly to the rack of oxygen bottles. Lifting one noiselessly from its cradle, she crept up behind Alvin, who was holding a fuse to the light. As she was about to strike he saw her shadow on the wall. He turned in time to see the blunt steel bottle coming at him. He raised his arm too late.

Ruth had meant to knock him unconscious with a blow to the back of his head. Instead, the bottle caught Alvin squarely between his eyes, shattering his steel-rimmed glasses. There was a sickening crunch of glass and bone, then he fell backward onto the machine and slid to the floor. Panting, Ruth stood over him, the bottle poised to strike again. Alvin did not move. Ruth hurled the weapon at the machine.

Fragile dials and switches shattered under the impact. The oxygen bottle fell and rolled across the floor, banging into the bench where Owen lay. Ruth retrieved it and began to attack the machine with a savage vengeance. When she was no longer strong enough to wield the bulky bottle, she dropped it and used her hands. As she ripped wires from their terminals, sparks flew in all directions and a cloud of brown acrid smoke issued from the battered control board. The machine hissed and spluttered like a dying deadly animal, bleeding molten steel and plastic to the floor. The thick, snakelike, silver conduit leading from the machine to the wall was smoldering.

Ruth paused to catch her breath. Panting, gulping air, she smiled at Owen with tear-glazed eyes and said, "He'll never hurt anybody again."

She took Owen's limp hand in hers. "Can you hear me now?" she asked.

Owen blinked.

"Do you understand what I'm saying?"

He blinked again.

"Try to talk. Can you?"

Slowly, agonizingly, Owen's lips formed a word,

194

which Ruth bent close to hear. The sound seemed to come from a great distance.

". . . Robin."

Ruth squeezed his hands, sobbed, and said, "I *knew* you wouldn't give up. I knew it just by your eyes. Remember when you looked in my eyes and told me all about myself? Well, when you were looking in my eyes I was looking in yours, Owen. They haven't changed."

Owen blinked both eyes, tried to smile.

"You're going to be all right, Owen. And then we'll go find your little boy."

She examined him, running her fingers tenderly over his body, removing sensors, wires, tape. She shuddered at the sight of his battered lacerated flesh. There was barely a part of him that was not bruised, cut, scratched, or burnt. Dried blood was streaked and smeared over his arms, back, chest, and legs. Wetting a towel in a small basin, she began to clean him.

As the drug overload in his system gradually lost its numbing and paralyzing effect, Owen began to feel her touch. He welcomed the return of pain. Pain, after senselessness, was like air to a drowning man, water to someone dying of thirst.

Behind Ruth, still sprawled on the floor, Alvin began to move. Gasping, moaning, he rolled to one side, holding his head. Blood seeped between his fingers and dripped on his white coat. Near him lay the bent and crumpled rims of his glasses. Mixed in the blood and gore that ran from his eye sockets were the shards of his shattered lenses. Groping blindly, he raised himself to his hands and knees and began to crawl, feeling his way toward the door.

Watching with horror, Owen tried to warn

Ruth, to shout her name. But he could only whisper it, and Ruth was too busy massaging life and sensation back into his legs to hear him.

"Ruth . . ."

Alvin's hands were on the doorknob, turning. Owen forced air through his throat. "Ruth!"

She put her ear close to his lips. "What?"

"Stop . . . him."

Ruth turned and saw Alvin, on his feet, staggering through the door. She ran for him but was too late. He slammed the door in her face. With clenched fists she beat on the thick metal, but the door was locked. She turned back to Owen, shaking her head, her red hair falling over her white coat, reminding Owen of fresh blood.

"I should have killed him," she said.

Owen shook his head, surprised that he could do it.

"That's not Alvin. Not the man I knew. He's a beast, Owen, and he'll be back."

Owen closed his eyes.

"Oh God, Owen, he'll bring the guards!"

"Help me, Ruth."

She put Owen's arms around her neck and pulled him to a sitting position. While she chafed and massaged his arms and legs, Owen watched the door.

"He's snapped, Owen. His mind's gone, I know that now. Last night I kept trying to reason with him, snap him out of it, bring him back. But he just got worse. He'd heard us up in my room, he knew you were there. And he knew you were still there when we left. He knew exactly where you were."

"I thought so."

"He put me in isolation and said he wouldn't

196

talk to me until I was ready to tell the truth. But I didn't want you to get caught, so I said nothing. I didn't know you were locked up."

In the corner the machine continued to hiss and spit sparks as its high currents continued to devour itself.

"I was so scared, Owen. I just prayed that everything would be all right in the morning. I fell asleep wondering what in the world was happening to him, to me, to this horrible little world I've been living in."

The lights went out. Ruth jumped, squeezed Owen's arm, whispered in his ear. "He's cut the power, Owen! He's coming back!"

They waited, listening, holding their breaths. When several minutes passed and nothing happened, Ruth went on with her massage and her story.

"When he woke me up this morning he was worse. He hadn't slept. He said he'd been up all night, helping the men with the funeral. He said he had you where he wanted you. Then he said if I didn't tell him the truth he'd keep me in that isolation cell forever. What's that smell?"

"I can't smell anything."

"I can. Something's burning."

"The machine."

"No, it's different now. Stronger."

"What did you tell him, Ruth?"

"I . . . I told him what I knew, what you told me."

"It's okay."

"I said your little boy had been kidnapped. I didn't say you suspected him, I just said you were looking for your little boy, in case he might have wandered in here. But he said that was a delusion you were having. He said you were really sick, dangerous, out of your mind. I told him you weren't sick at all, and he slapped me. He went away, left me there, frightened to death. I was there alone all day. Then he came to get me. He made me promise to help him, to do anything he said. He said we were going to help you, Owen, make you stop suffering. When I first saw you lying there I almost believed him. Something's definitely burning, Owen."

"I can smell it now."

"Can you stand up? Want to try?"

With one arm around Ruth, Owen stood and walked slowly, feeling his way around the bench in the darkness. A strong, acrid odor filled his nostrils.

"Not much longer, Ruth. I'm weak as a baby, but I'm going to be all right."

"Owen, it's getting hard to breathe."

"It's a fire, Ruth. Electrical fire. The machine's shorting out the wires inside the walls."

"Owen, we're trapped!"

"We'll make it. Get down on the floor where the air's better."

Owen and Ruth crawled under the bench, holding each other as the room filled with toxic smoke.

"I'm so scared, Owen. I just don't know what's happening."

"Don't be frightened. We're going to survive this, just like everything else."

"Oh God, Owen, take me out of here."

"I will."

"You said you would, Owen. I said I'd help you and you said you'd help me."

"I will, don't worry. Everything's going to work out, you'll see."

"Owen, when . . . when we get your little boy back . . . and we're out of here forever . . . will you let me stay with you a little while?"

"Sure. You can stay as long as you want."

"I can barely breathe, Owen."

"Lie down. Face me. Breathe real easy, Ruth."

"You'd take me in, Owen? Crazy as I am?"

"I'll take you in. And you're not crazy and you never were. If it weren't for you, I'd be an imbecile by now."

Suddenly a key clicked in the lock and the door swung open. A husky voice, filled with panic, shouted, "Fire! Everybody out! Dr. Alvin? You in here, Dr. Alvin?" It was Mahoney. They heard him curse, then move down the hall, unlocking doors, shouting, "Fire!"

"Come on, Ruth," Owen said, his strength gradually returning. "Let's go get my boy."

"Where does he live, Ruth? Which way?"

"Follow me."

Outside the soundproofed room now, they could hear shouts and screams from above. There were explosive sounds of men running, slamming doors, shattering windows, and furniture. Then, from a doorway, they heard a shout for help: the voice was Rupert's. Owen rushed into the bare room, recognizing it as the one he'd shared with Rupert earlier that day. And there, huddled in a corner, still bound by the straitjacket, was Rupert.

"Help me up, Owen!" he shouted. "Place is burning down!"

"Rupert," said Owen, helping the young man to his feet. "I thought you were dead. They told me—"

"They told me the same thing about you, Owen. I didn't believe them for a minute."

"But I heard the dog on you—"

"They shot it! Just after they stuck the needle in you. They must have had it all planned."

"You're all right?"

"I'll be all right when I get this goddamn thing off me."

Ruth hugged her brother, sweeping his red hair from his eyes. "We're going, Rupert! We're getting out of here soon as we find his little boy."

"We better find him fast, Owen. This place is going to come down on our heads." Rupert stared at the low ceiling, now covered with thin yellow smoke.

Owen put his arms around Ruth and Rupert, guiding them down the hallway.

"Here," said Ruth, stopping at a door at the end of the corridor. She turned the knob, whispered, "It's locked."

"Knock."

"Owen," she whispered, "he could have a gun."

"I don't think it would do him any good, Ruth. Knock."

Ruth knocked three times.

"Yes?" Alvin's voice was hollow, toneless.

"Alvin, it's Ruth. Can I come in?"

They heard someone groping, stumbling toward the door; then came the sound of locks snapping open, bolts clicking back, the door opening on stiff and rusted hinges. In the pale light from a small basement window stood the director, one bloody hand over his sightless eyes. His other hand held a dripping paintbrush. Staring straight ahead, he tried to smile.

"I wanted a little more time, Ruth," he said, "but I guess it's as ready as it'll ever be."

"What, Alvin?"

"The surprise I told you about. Come in, Ruth. Look around. I hope you like it."

Suddenly Ruth realized the damage she had done. Her trembling hands went out to him, but Owen took them in his own and guided her into the room. Rupert went to the window, pulled back the curtains. It was unbarred, but too small for them to climb through. Alvin stood in the middle of the room, dropping his paintbrush to the floor.

"How do you like the color?" he asked.

The rough concrete walls still showed through a thin coat of light blue paint. The ceiling was painted white, the floor carpeted in a soft gray. In the little window set high in the wall were ivy and cactus plants in colorful plastic pots. The furniture—a divan and two easy chairs—was new, covered in white imitation leather. In one corner was a Formica-topped dining table with white candles in plastic candlesticks. Around it were three chairs. Pale blue paint from Alvin's brush was splattered everywhere, giving the otherwise neat and orderly room a crazed appearance.

"I did it myself, Ruth. Nobody helped me."

Owen looked at Ruth, put a finger to his lips.

"It's lovely, Alvin."

"The color is all right?"

"It's perfect."

"The room looks larger, I think," he said.

"Much larger."

"I . . . I'm having some difficulty seeing, Ruth. Do you think it has to do with my accident?"

". . . Yes."

"It will pass?"

"Of course," she said, shooting a painful glance at Owen. She put her head on Alvin's chest and hugged him while he stroked her hair.

Rupert pressed close to Owen, whispered, "Owen, we got to get the hell out of here, fast!"

A tremendous crash from above was followed by the sound of shattering glass.

"What's that noise, Ruth?" Alvin asked. "Is everything all right upstairs? Mahoney was very upset about something."

"Everything's all right, Alvin. But tell me," she said, looking around her, "where's the rest of the surprise? You said you had something special."

"In there," he said, indicating a door near the table. "In the bedroom."

Owen turned the knob, opened the door and rushed in. His eyes fastened on a large, new, color television set, its screen a blank. It sat on a low table before a double bed with a newly upholstered headboard and several large shiny cushions. In the middle of the bed, squatting on a white bedspread, was the Doberman puppy. The dog looked at Owen, growled, and dashed under the bed. When Owen bent to look, the dog leaped to a bureau and from there to a small open window, jumping through.

Owen searched everywhere—the darkened corners, a closet, a small bathroom. Nothing. When he returned, Alvin was on his knees before Ruth, trembling, squeezing and kissing her hands.

"He's *ours*, Ruth! Our own little boy. Go in and see him."

Owen caught Ruth's eye and shook his head.

"Where did he come from?" Ruth asked.

"I found him all alone—abandoned and lost. A gift from God! Ruth, he's the answer to all our prayers. And he needs us so much. Isn't it wonderful?"

Rupert nudged Owen with his shoulder, nodding toward the table where a key ring lay. Owen found the key to the padlock on Rupert's straitjacket. While he fumbled with it, Rupert whispered, "Owen, we've got about a minute to get out of here. When the roof goes we're done."

"Robin?" called Alvin. "Robin, come out here, please? There's someone here to see you."

"There's no one in the bedroom, Alvin," said Ruth.

"There isn't?"

Owen rushed back to the bedroom and parted the curtains of the little window the dog had run through. Outside, the grounds of Mizpah were bathed in an eerie light. It was evening and the blazing building threw vaporous nightmare shadows on the white wall beyond. Excited inmates, shivering with fear and rage, were huddled in groups. Watching the fire, they moaned, wailed, and swayed. Owen saw no guards, no one he recognized except for the black-bearded lunatic, Cebulski, who was waving something that looked like gardener's shears.

Owen examined the window. It was unbarred and opened wide. It was small, too small for a man, but just large enough for the puppy—or Robin—to slip through.

Owen scratched his head, looked at the bed. Robin had passed the day watching television. When the power went off the set went dead. Robin had gone outside.

To play.

"Let's go," ordered Owen on his way from the

bedroom. The air was beginning to fill with dark smoke.

"Who's here, Ruth?" asked Alvin.

"Friends. There's a fire, Alvin. We have to get out."

"My God," exclaimed Rupert, "I can hardly move my arms!" Painfully he held his arms before him, wincing as sensation returned.

Owen threw open the door and was engulfed in smoke. "Hold hands!" he shouted, taking Ruth's hand and pulling her behind him. Ruth held Alvin's hand and Rupert clung to his coat. Coughing and gagging, they fought their way down the smoke-filled hallway while above them beams crashed and men screamed. Not everyone, Owen guessed, had been released, and it was too late now.

Nearly overcome by the dense smoke, Owen found the stairway and climbed. At the top the massive oak door stood open, fresh air rushing in, fanning the flames that consumed the upper floors. Stumbling blindly, they ran clear of the building.

When Owen could see he stopped to get his bearings. Not far from him he saw a mob of frantic, gibbering inmates standing in a circle around something on the ground. They were kicking someone, stomping and jumping up and down on a figure that barely moved. Owen saw a bloody kitchen knife rise above the heads of the crowd and come down. He heard a sharp scream, followed by the insane and vacant laughter of the men.

"Dr. Alvin!" someone called, running up to the director, who stood with his head bent, one hand over his sightless eyes. It was Mahoney, frightened, brandishing his revolver.

"They got Welles and Trinning!" screamed the guard. "What should I do?"

At that moment Mahoney was stabbed from behind by two men creeping from the shadows. They howled, dragging the heavyset guard away. Owen's heart skipped a beat when he saw a filthy hand rip the pistol from Mahoney's clutching fingers. Six shots followed as the big revolver barked above the roar of the fire, and Mahoney's bloody body went limp. The inmates, giving full vent to their blood lust, began to look for other victims.

"Where's the kid?" someone screamed.

"Get the kid, get the kid!" they shouted.

"Follow me!" Owen ordered, leading his group around a corner of the building. In the distance was the old Cadillac, big and black, untouched by the flames. Owen's mind formed a plan. Dragging the others, he began to run. As he did he heard the shouts of the inmates, hard on their heels.

Clutching Alvin's ring of keys, Owen jerked open the car's front door and jumped behind the wheel. Ruth scrambled into the backseat, followed by Rupert, who dragged Alvin by his coat. Rupert was trying to close the door when hands reached in and tore Alvin from his grasp.

"Where's the kid? Where's the kid?" they demanded, closing in on the blind man.

Alvin raised his arms, silencing the inmates. "Boys," he said, "I want no more of this behavior! We're dealing with an emergency here, and—"

"Give us the kid, you monster!" screamed Patruzi, the small monkey-faced man who had turned on Owen the night before.

"The kid, you son of a bitch!" screamed another.

"Boys," yelled Alvin, his voice cracking, "if you will behave yourselves—" He was given no time to finish. They picked him up, lifted him high above their heads. Then, in a mad rush, they ran him toward a blazing stairwell and flung him in.

Owen could not find the ignition key. While he fumbled, squinting in the near darkness, Ruth and Rupert hugged each other in the backseat, unable to believe their eyes. Ruth screamed in horror, covered her eyes. Owen looked up in time to see Alvin rush from the flames, his white hair and white coat in flames. The men laughed hysterically as the blind man ran in circles, tearing at his burning body. They grabbed him and threw him back in the fiery hole. They waited, and when he did not emerge, they ran toward the Cadillac.

"Rip them, tear them!" shrieked a short fat idiot who wielded an ice pick before him, pointing it at the car. At that moment Owen found the key and turned it in the lock. Pumping the accelerator and praying, he heard the tired old battery turn the big engine over once, twice, then stop. He turned the key again and the engine groaned, clicked, and belched gasoline vapor. Flooded.

A jabbering inmate leaped onto the hood of the car and tried to smash the windshield with his forehead. A dozen inmates swarmed around the car.

"Get the girl," shouted Cebulski, smashing a headlight with his shears. "Get Ruth Sooey!"

"Sooey, Sooey, Sooey!" shouted a fool in bloody pajamas. "Get her and fuck her and eat her raw!"

A grisly face appeared in the open window next to Owen. Matted stringy hair fell in ringlets over a furrowed doglike brow. An imbecilic mouth, drooling saliva, opened wide and screamed, *"Where's that little boy?"*

Owen punched the face and rolled up the window. He tried again to start the engine, but it was still flooded. Behind him Ruth screamed, "Owen, watch out!"

A long, crudely fashioned knife plunged suddenly through the convertible top, just missing the top of Owen's head. More men jumped to the flimsy roof and tried to tear it away with their hands. More knives stabbed the old canvas, just missing Ruth and Rupert, huddled low in the backseat.

"Get the girl!"

"Find the kid!"

"We'll fuck the girl! We'll all fuck her!"

Ruth saw a filthy arm reach through a rent in the roof and grope in the darkness for her hair. The hand, swooping down at her, found her face. Ruth bit it and it was drawn quickly away. In the front seat Owen cursed the tired battery, the flooded carburetor.

They were moving! Looking back, Owen saw a throng of giggling men pushing the old car toward the burning building. He steered away, rounded the building and saw the front gate in the distance. The men kept pushing, rocking the car, pounding on the metal and glass, shouting horrible threats and crude obscenities.

Owen recognized Welter, the trusty who had left him locked in the little attic room. Welter was having a furious argument with another inmate, both of them fighting over something round that hung from Welter's hand. They failed to see the Cadillac rolling noiselessly toward them. Owen did not brake. Both men were felled from behind, crushed beneath the wheels. Owen saw the object they had been fighting over roll from Welter's lifeless hand: a human head, long-haired and oozing gore.

They were a hundred yards from the gate when Owen saw something that made him step on the brake, snap on the remaining headlight. Caught in one weak yellow beam, two small figures turned abruptly and headed for the gates.

"Shut up, everybody," shouted Cebulski, pointing toward the figures. "Look over there!"

Owen turned off the headlight, too late. Running for their lives across the fire-lighted lawn were a puppy and a little boy.

"The kid!" screamed a man who stood by Owen's door. "Don't let him get away!"

Owen moved quickly. Kicking open the door, he sent it smashing into the closest man. Over his shoulder he shouted to Rupert, "Either get the car started, Rupert, or run like hell!"

With the bloodthirsty mob at his heels Owen raced across the lawn toward his son, shouting his name. Halfway to him he saw the puppy scoot between the bars. The boy tried to follow, but could not. Like a trapped animal he turned to face the rushing crowd of madmen.

Arriving well before the mob, Owen scooped the boy into his arms and hugged him. The child resisted, then looked closely into his father's face.

"Daddy?" Robin's face was filled with fear and uncertainty.

"Robin, it's me, it's daddy."

"Daddy!" screamed Robin. "Look behind you!"

Over his shoulder Owen saw the lunatic horde closing in for the kill, screaming, *"Eat the kid! Drink his blood!"*

Hugging Robin with one arm, Owen began to climb the rusty bars. He was halfway to the top when he felt rough hands grab his heels. He kicked them away, inching toward the sharp spikes at the top. The spikes curved inward, toward the asylum, and Owen realized that with only one free arm he would not be able to climb over them.

A few feet below him the men screamed and cackled, slashing the air with knives. "Give us the kid!" they shouted. "Give us the little bastard!"

"Robin, can you hang on to my neck?"

"I'll try, daddy."

Robin put his thin arms around his father's neck, joined his fingers and hung on. Owen released his grasp slowly, praying that Robin had the strength to hang on for the moment or two it would take to clear the spikes. Robin's hold was choking him, but it didn't matter; in a moment or two they would be free.

Owen's hands were on the spikes, his body dangling, when Robin screamed, "Daddy!" and fell. The crowd of inmates roared as Robin landed in their waiting arms. With a scream of rage Owen turned, released his grip, and plunged onto the heads of the throng. Locking his arms around his son, he rolled to the ground, looking for a clearing among the kicking legs, the flashing knives.

He felt a sharp pain in his buttock and knew he had been stabbed. Rolling free, he found his feet and ran blindly into the concrete wall. His head smacked the cement and he fell to his knees. Behind him the men laughed with glee. Something wet landed on his back and shoulders, soaking the torn pajama bottoms he still wore. Even with his head reeling and dazed he identified the liquid they had thrown at him: gasoline.

"Matches!" someone shouted. "Light the matches!"

"Burn 'em, burn 'em!"

"Make 'em dance!"

Holding Robin like an infant, Owen stood and faced the men. He saw half a dozen matches burning in the inmates' fingers and the manic stare in the inmates' eyes. Suddenly, above their clamor, he shouted, "I've been to the *Bad* Room!"

"What?" asked a voice.

Owen took a step toward the crowd. Men backed away, giggling, ready to attack. "I've been in the Bad Room all day and *nothing* can hurt me now!" He took another step.

"The *Bad* Room!" said somebody.

"He's *bad,*" yelled someone else.

Owen took another step. "I took twenty thousand volts, boys, and that's *bad.*"

"*Bad!*"

"He's BAD!"

"He's very, very SICK!"

Then some idiot threw his match.

Owen's head had cleared and he was running when the match set him on fire. It took him a few seconds to reach the small reflecting pond and another few seconds to put out the flames. His flesh was burned, but not badly. Robin was untouched. When Owen looked up he saw that he was trapped.

The shallow pond, some thirty feet in diameter, was surrounded by his tormentors. In whatever direction he turned they were there waiting for him at the edge of the pool. Laughing, jeering at him, waiting for him to make a move.

The blazing madhouse was reflected on the pond's black surface. Flames, blue and orange, shimmered and cavorted around Owen and the boy, who turned in a slow circle, looking for escape. As Owen stood there, holding his son on his shoulder and catching his breath, the men began to dance.

> Dance with the dolly with the
>   hole in her stocking, hole in her stocking,
>   hole in her stocking.
> Dance with the dolly with the
>   hole in her stocking,
> Dance by the light of the moon!

Shuffling, slapping their thighs and knees, the madmen danced like primitives around a bonfire. They danced jigs, spinning and laughing, pointing at Owen and making horrible faces. Owen noticed that none of them had stepped over the pond's rim into the stagnant, knee-deep water.

A tremendous crash was followed by the wind's roar as the asylum's great tiled roof caved in on the burning rafters and fell through the charred floors below. Firelight played in the windows of the walls that were still standing. Fire gutted everything that would burn.

Owen's terror mounted as an inmate stepped into the water. Kicking up his feet, splashing playfully, he beckoned to the rest. Knee-deep and wading in a wide circle around Owen and Robin, he was followed by another man, and another, and the ring closed slowly.

> Dance with the dolly, with the dolly,
>   with the dolly . . .

211

"We'll throw 'em in the fire and roast 'em!"

"We'll eat the kid!"

"Him too! He's been *bad!*"

"Been to the *Bad* Room!"

"Stick 'em, stick 'em!"

"I want their *heads!*"

"Chew their toes off!"

"Drink blood!"

"Blood, blood, BLOOD!"

"Jesus, Jesus, JESUS!"

"Oh, get them, GET THEM!"

Just as the inmates closed for a final attack, the Cadillac, driven by Rupert, crashed through the crowd, its hood and bumper acting like a battering ram on the frenzied psychopaths. Owen saw the car stop, the rear door swing open over the lip of the pool. Carrying Robin like a football and straight-arming men who stood in his way, Owen charged for the car. Diving headlong into the backseat, he scrambled to close the door behind him. Frustrated and enraged, the men swarmed like ants over the car as Rupert moved forward, picking up speed, mowing down and mashing the bodies of the men in his path.

Rupert dodged a knife thrust, the wicked point glancing off a visor, just missing his cheek. With a whoop he spun the wheel, stepped heavily on the gas, and yelled back to Owen, "First time I ever drove a car!"

Spilling inmates, the big car slid heavily into the concrete steps of the asylum and bounced off. Men were running toward the car from all directions, howling and waving weapons. Patruzi clung to the hood, shaking his fist at Rupert and Ruth, waiting for his chance to hurl himself through the gaping holes in the convertible's top.

But Rupert didn't give him that chance. He spun the car by the gutted building just as a massive towering chimney collapsed in a spray of brick, flames, and sparks, falling onto the heads of men running after the car. Rupert sped across the low meadow of parched weeds, flattened a rotting cherry tree, and kept going.

"Hey, Owen, I can't see a thing!"

"Turn on your headlights!"

"I tried. They're bashed out! What do we do?"

"There's only one way out, Rupert," said Ruth.

"Go for the gates," said Owen.

As Rupert turned the wheel, the white wall loomed up before them, the rear of the car just missing the grave that Owen and Rupert had opened that morning. Owen saw it, shivered, and hugged Robin, who was rigid with fear.

When Owen looked up they were moving at high speed over rough ground, headed for the gates. Throwing himself over his son, he fell to the floor of the car. From the front seat he heard Rupert say, "Hang on everybody, we're in the hands of God."

Patruzi, standing on the front bumper and hanging on to the hood ornament, did not see the gates in time. The massive old car slammed into the gates at eighty, tearing them from their rusted hinges and flinging them into the pines. Patruzi's body, squashed to a pulp like a bug on a windshield, slid from the hood in a gory trail and was gone.

The Cadillac left the road, plowed through dense brush and scrawny trees, then found gravel again. Rupert slowed the car to a crawl, making his way slowly down the narrow road that led back to Sooey's bar.

Owen raised his head and looked back. The old asylum was reduced to a pile of brick and glowing ashes. It had burned to the ground and no firemen had come. The rangers, secure in their watchtower, had simply and happily watched the place burn down.

A moment later, Rupert slammed on the brakes, grinding the car to a stop. "Look," he said, "there's that little dog."

Ruth swung open her door. "Here, pup, come here puppy. . . ."

Owen and Robin looked at each other as the dog jumped in, sat on Ruth's lap, and licked her face. Ruth laughed, hugged the dog, and said, "I *like* this little dog."

"It ran away, daddy," said Robin, "when you were in the bar. I tried to catch him, but he wouldn't let me."

"Did you go in the woods, son?"

"No, I walked down a road. Then it got dark and I got lost."

"What happened then?" Owen asked as the car began to move.

"A car stopped. The man said he'd take me home and wait for you to come and get me. You took a long time, daddy."

Owen squeezed his little boy. "I'm sorry I took so long, son."

"What were you doing?"

"I'll tell you someday. Were you scared?"

"I was watching TV."

"The whole time?"

"All night and all day, till it went off. I missed you, daddy."

"I missed you too, Robie."

"You know what, daddy?"

"What?"

"I hate TV."

Owen patted Robin's hand.

"I kept asking the man when you were coming, daddy. You know what he said?"

"What?"

"He said maybe you weren't coming. He said maybe you were tired of me."

"He told you that?"

"He said maybe you weren't looking for me at all."

"Well, what did you say?"

Robin smiled, yawned, and put his arms around his father's neck.

"I told him he was crazy."

Tears formed in Owen's eyes as he buried his face in Robin's soft hair.

"I love you, daddy," Robin whispered, so that no one else would hear.

"I love you, Robin. God, how I love you."

The camper was parked beside Sooey's Bar just as Owen had left it, windows down, doors unlocked. The keys were gone, but there was a spare set under the floor mat. Owen put Robin on the seat beside him, and Ruth climbed in next to the boy, the little Doberman nestled in her arms. Owen started the engine and looked at Rupert.

"Want to come with us, Rupert?"

Rupert looked up and down Zion Road. "I better not, Owen," he said. "I better stick around, see how Dusty's doing."

"She can take care of herself," said Ruth. "Why don't we stick together?"

"She's not strong like she was, Ruth. I better stay."

Owen extended his hand. "Rupert, I've been through hell. All I can say is thank God you were there."

"Amen," said Rupert.

"Burma Shave," said Owen.

As Owen put the camper in gear the little dog suddenly jumped from Ruth's arms and leaped out the window. It barked twice, then ran into the woods.

"I'll get it," said Rupert.

"Wait a minute." Owen turned to Robin. "You want that dog?"

Robin shook his head.

Owen smiled at Rupert. "The hell with it."

They were ten miles from Mizpah when the first fire truck whizzed by. Owen cut his speed, calmed down, and thought things over.

They were going to make it. In a little while they would be out of the Pines, over the Delaware and in another state. In time his wounds would heal and the long nightmare would come to an end. He'd get back to work, maybe start a new thirty-footer, and try to forget what he'd been through.

Ruth would get a new start. There were things she could do in the boatyard, places around Seabright where she could sit and watch the ocean, breathe fresh air, and find a new way to face life.

Robin was shaken, but he'd pull through. Maybe he'd forget Mizpah, forgive his parents, find himself. Maybe the whole ghastly experience would help Robin become a normal happy child again.

Another fire truck flew by. Owen cracked a smile. Everything was going to be all right.

Just then he heard a strange sound. The engine was running smoothly. The radio was off. Ruth was asleep, her head against the window, hands in her lap. Then he saw Robin.

The boy was wide awake, talking. He rocked back and forth, staring at his father, his lips forming words, his voice a hiss. Owen leaned close and heard his son whisper:

Dance with the dolly with the hole in her stocking, hole in her stocking, hole in . . .

Owen stopped smiling and stepped on the gas.

"Michael McDowell's best book yet...He is one of the best writers of horror in this country."
—Peter Straub

MICHAEL McDOWELL'S
CONTINUING SAGA OF THE CASKEY FAMILY.
BLACKWATER

BLACKWATER, an epic novel of horror, will appear serially for six months beginning in January 1983 with completion in June. Michael McDowell, described by Stephen King as "the finest writer of paperback originals in America," is at the height of his storytelling prowess as he tells of the powers exerted by the mysterious Elinor Dammert over the citizens of Perdido, Alabama. Her ghastly, inexplicable ability to use water to gain her hideous ends is a recurring and mystifying pattern.

THE FLOOD (January)
THE LEVEE (February)
THE HOUSE (March)

THE WAR (April)
THE FORTUNE (May)
RAIN (June)

AVON BOOKS

Available wherever paperbacks are sold, or directly from the publisher. Include 50¢ per copy for postage and handling; allow 6-8 weeks for delivery. Avon Books. Mail Order Dept., 224 West 57th St., N.Y., N.Y. 10019.

Blackwater 2-83